***"There's something about you."
Her eyes held him. "I can't explain it,
but you make me feel like...like I've been
waiting for you forever."***

Had she waited? He had no right to expect her to have. He had no right to ask.

"Have you been?"

"I don't know." Her brow crinkled. "What is it that people wait for, Clark?"

He crushed her mouth with a kiss.

He whispered, "Lilleth..." in her ear. He kissed her again, this time slowly savoring her.

"Well," she murmured at last, when he allowed her a breath. "You've just made it clear to me that in some ways I am still a virgin." She curled her fingers into his shirt. "Come with me into the bedroom, Clark."

* * *

Rebel with a Heart
Harlequin® Historical #1160—November 2013

Author Note

Are you like I am? Does your heart beat a little faster for a mysterious hero?

When I was eight years old I sat in front of the television set and fell madly, completely in love with Zorro/ Don Diego. The humor of the Don made me laugh, but when the dashing protector emerged I melted. I carried that torch for a few years and, to be honest, there's still a bit of the flame left.

Who can resist the lure of Superman/Clark Kent? Or Batman/Bruce Wayne? For me, the hero in disguise is an irresistible character.

For the longest time I've wanted to create one of my own. I hope you enjoy reading about Trace Ballentine/ Clark Clarkly, and that just maybe your heart will beat a little faster.

Three cheers for heroes in disguise!

Best wishes and happy reading.

REBEL WITH
A HEART

CAROL ARENS

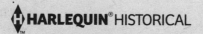

HARLEQUIN® HISTORICAL

Recycling programs
for this product may
not exist in your area.

ISBN-13: 978-0-373-29760-3

REBEL WITH A HEART

Copyright © 2013 by Carol Arens

HARLEQUIN®
www.Harlequin.com

Printed in U.S.A.

To my daughter, Jennifer Lynne, because sometimes life takes a turn and grants you a miracle.

CAROL ARENS

While in the third grade, Carol Arens had a teacher who noted that she ought to spend less time daydreaming and looking out the window and more time on her sums. Today, Carol spends as little time on sums as possible. Daydreaming about plots and characters is still far more interesting to her.

As a young girl, she read books by the dozen. She dreamed that one day she would write a book of her own. A few years later, Carol set her sights on a new dream. She wanted to be the mother of four children. She was blessed with a son, then three daughters. While raising them she never forgot her goal of becoming a writer. When her last child went to high school she purchased a big old clunky word processor and began to type out a story.

She joined Romance Writers of America, where she met generous authors who taught her the craft of writing a romance novel. With the knowledge she gained, she sold her first book and saw her lifelong dream come true.

Carol lives with her real-life hero husband, Rick, in Southern California, where she was born and raised. She feels blessed to be doing what she loves, with all her children and a growing number of perfect and delightful grandchildren living only a few miles from her front door.

When she is not writing, reading or playing with her grandchildren, Carol loves making trips to the local nursery. She delights in scanning the rows of flowers, envisaging which pretty plants will best brighten her garden.

She enjoys hearing from readers, and invites you to contact her at carolsarens@yahoo.com.

Chapter One

Riverwalk, South Dakota
November, 1879

A splinter jutting from the boardwalk pierced Trace Ballentine's trousers. He cursed his luck. He growled at fate. How could it be possible that he was facing one of the most pivotal moments of his life with a piece of wood stabbing his rump?

Admittedly, he hadn't slipped by accident, but he hadn't intended to take a woman down with him, either. Still, here the lady was, sprawled across his lap in front of the ticket counter at the train depot, with the contents of her valise scattered near and far. Undergarments and shoes, ribbons and hatpins littered the boardwalk, mostly crushed under the stack of books he had been carrying.

He snatched his shattered spectacles from under his knee and plopped them on his nose.

Even through a spiderweb of broken glass he knew this woman. Even after sixteen years of foggy memory and change he recognized his one true love.

"Why, you big…" She seemed to be searching for the nastiest word in her vocabulary.

"Oaf?" he supplied.

"Dolt."

The accusation didn't sting; she'd called him worse dozens of times in playfulness. Still, that didn't mean he wasn't wounded to his soul.

Lilleth Grace Preston stared straight into his eyes without knowing who he was.

In every fantasy he'd ever had of their miraculous reunion they had showered tears and kisses all over each other.

He had vowed to love her forever, and damned if he hadn't. He'd cherished her memory since he was fourteen years old, yet not a twitch of her eyebrow or a blink of her lashes revealed that she recalled him.

To be fair, how could he have expected her to? The last time they had been together he had been gangly, whereas now he was tall and filled out. Over the years his hair had darkened from blond to brown. These days he wore a beard, trimmed short and neat. Back then he had barely sprouted peach fuzz.

He was nothing like the boy he had been, while she looked very much the same. With her red curls, snapping blue eyes and mouth that went from a grimace to a smile in a flash, he'd have known her even if he hadn't been cursed with a mind that remembered nearly everything.

"Kindly remove your person from under me, Mr....?" She arched one brow.

It's me. It's Trace.

"Clark," he declared. He wrinkled his brow, then added a hiccup.

"Mr. Clark, your—"

"Clarkly, that is. Mr. Clark Clarkly, at your service, miss."

"Mr. Clark Clarkly, kindly remove your knee from my bustle."

"Your...? Oh, my word, I beg your pardon." He straightened his leg and reached for her hand, desperate for just one touch, even if that touch was through a leather glove.

She allowed him to help her to her feet. He then made a show of being a buffoon by attempting to straighten her skirt.

Curse it, he *was* a buffoon, and he didn't even have to act a part. Of all the disguises he could have chosen for this assignment, why did it have to be Clark Clarkly?

Had he ever dreamed that he might run into Lilleth Preston he'd have made himself a lawman or a cowboy. Anyone but good old Clarkly, the bungling, bookish librarian.

But Trace was good and stuck now. Most of the citizens of Riverwalk had made the acquaintance of

Clarkly—run into him, quite literally. He couldn't change identities midassignment. Too much was at stake. The innocent inmates at the Hanispree Mental Hospital depended on Clarkly.

He ought to thank his lucky stars that Lilleth hadn't recognized him. It broke his heart, but it was for the best.

Hot damn, he was stuck in a muddle of his own making with no way out. There was nothing for it but to dive in headfirst.

Lilleth slapped his hand where it attempted to straighten that fascinating, if tweaked, little bustle behind her skirt.

"Mr. Clarkly! Have you no shame?"

Good girl, Lils, he thought, *you still hold your own against anyone.*

"Why…yes. Usually, that is. Miss, you pack quite a wallop." He shook his slapped hand, then stooped to gather her belongings from under his books.

She would think he was an idiot for plucking up her lacy, pink-ribboned corset, but that was as close to intimacy as he was likely ever to get with her.

Lilleth crouched beside him, her hand already in motion to deliver another swat. He shoved the garment at her, but not before he noticed that it smelled like roses.

"Don't you lay a finger on those bloomers." Lilleth leveled a glare at him, snatched up her belongings and stuffed them into her valise. She snapped it closed, then stood up.

November wind, blowing in the promise of the first snow, swirled the hem of Lilleth's skirt. Her toe tapped the boardwalk with the one-two-three-pause, one-two-three-pause rhythm that he remembered. She was struggling with her temper.

He gathered up his books and, in true Clark style, layered them in alphabetical order. He'd intended her to notice that, and she had. She rolled her eyes and sighed.

"It has been a pleasure, truly." He offered his hand. "I'm sorry about the little knock-you-down. My deepest apologies, and welcome to Riverwalk."

Most women wouldn't accept his apology, given that he'd been clumsy upon stupid upon rude, but he left his hand extended just in case.

Lilleth stared at his face for a long time, studying, weighing, judging.

"I'm ever so sorry, Miss...?"

"Well, accidents do happen, after all." She shook his hand. The smile that had haunted his dreams pardoned him. "I'm Lilly Gordon."

Gordon? Married? No! Sixteen years ago she had taken his hand, pressed it to her twelve-year-old heart and vowed to marry him and only him.

"Hey, Ma, Mary's getting hungry."

A boy, no more than ten years old, walked up to Lilly Gordon carrying a baby.

"Cold, too," the boy added, frowning and shooting Clark an assessing look.

The baby didn't appear to be hungry or cold. In fact, it was bundled against the chill so that only a pair of blue eyes—Lils's eyes—and a pert little nose peeked out.

Trace admired the boy for stepping up. Some big galoot had just knocked his mother down.

"Make Mr. Clarkly's acquaintance, Jess." Lilleth took the baby from the boy's arms. "Then we'll be on our way. There's the hotel, just up ahead."

"A pleasure to meet you, young man," he said. And it was, too, now that the shock was wearing off. He extended his hand.

The boy cocked his head, studied his face as his mother had done, and then, like her, made up his mind in an instant. He shook Clark's hand.

"Well, good day, then, Mr. Clarkly," Lilleth said.

A spray of red curls tumbled out from under her hat. Her smile warmed him in places that hadn't been warm in forever.

Jess picked up his mother's valise, his own, and carried a smaller one tucked under his arm.

Trace watched Lilleth and her little family walk toward the Riverwalk Hotel. It was a good thing it was so close, for the temperature seemed to be dropping by the minute.

He was proud of Lils. She had grown to be a fine and beautiful woman. Even with a baby riding her hip the sway of her gait would be enough to catch any man's eye.

It was a lucky thing for him that she was married.

He had his mission, one he was dedicated to. Mrs. Gordon had her family. Life would go on.

Yes, it was very lucky that she was married. He hadn't really thought Lilleth would remain his Lils forever. Everyone grew up, everyone changed. No one remained a child forever. Not him, and most certainly not the lovely woman walking away from him.

Lilly Gordon glanced back. She arched one brow and smiled with the shadow of a question crossing her face.

He gripped his armload of alphabetized books tight.

It's me, Lils. It's Trace.

Blessed heat poured from the fireplace in the lobby of the Riverwalk Hotel. Lilleth walked past the check-in desk, pointing Jess toward the big hearth.

November in South Dakota was a beast.

"Sit there, Jess." She pointed to a big padded chair, one of a pair flanking the fireplace. "Get your sister out of that blanket so the warmth can reach her."

Lilleth removed her coat and gloves. She stood before the fire, letting it warm her, front then back. It took a few moments, but the bitter cold finally quit her bones.

She glanced about, relieved to see the hotel lobby

empty of patrons. Through an open door to her right she heard the ting of utensils against plates. An aroma of fresh warm bread swirled throughout the lobby, mixing with the scent of burning wood.

The moment she checked into her room, she would take the children to the dining room for dinner. They had to be hungry. The strenuous travel they had been forced to endure left little time for leisurely meals.

Riverwalk in November was not a place she would choose to be, but choice had been taken from her some time ago.

The hotel clerk bent down behind the tall counter. Lilleth took that moment to attempt to straighten her bustle. It had been crushed and bent beyond repair. No amount of yanking or pulling made a whit of difference to its appearance.

By all rights Mr. Clark Clarkly ought to pay for it. The man was beyond clumsy. Thank goodness it hadn't been Jess he had bowled over. He and Mary might have been injured. Mr. Clarkly ought to take his stroll with a warning to fellow pedestrians tied about his neck.

But there was something about him…something almost familiar. She couldn't at this very second imagine what it was, though.

"I'll be back, Jess. I'm going to check in, then we'll get something to eat."

Frigid wind huffed against the windowpanes, but

the hotel lobby was lovely and warm. Thank the stars that she had been able to wire ahead and get reservations on short notice.

"Good afternoon, Mr. Green." Lilleth read his name from the plaque on the counter. "My name is Lilly Gordon. I'd like to register for my room, if you please."

Mr. Green looked her over with interest, as men tended to do. It was a fact of life that nature and her mother had bequeathed her a figure that attracted men's attention. She had quit taking offense to their reactions years before. Men were men, after all, for good or ill.

"Mr. Green?" she asked, returning his attention to her face. "My room?"

The man blushed, ran his thumb down a list of names on the hotel register and then frowned.

"That's Mrs. Gordon," Lilleth said, feeling uneasy. The clerk ought to be smiling and handing her a key by now. "Mrs. Lilly Gordon."

He clicked his tongue against his teeth, then ran his forefinger over the register one more time. Halfway down, his finger stopped. He withdrew a pair of spectacles from his pocket, placed them on his nose, then bent low to peer at the page.

Lilleth tapped her foot.

Mr. Green closed the book and pressed his long, thin fingers on top of it. He cleared his throat.

"I do apologize, Mrs. Gordon. There appears to have been a mistake."

"Kindly check again." Tap tap, tap. "My reservation was confirmed."

"I see that, yes." The man shifted his weight. "But it appears that your room has been given to someone else."

Lilleth took a breath, slowly and calmly. She let it out, drawing deep down for a smile. *You catch more men with lace than you do with homespun*, she reminded herself. This philosophy was also something bequeathed by her mother.

"I'm sure you can provide them another room. Certainly they will understand once you explain the mistake."

"I'd like nothing more, Mrs. Gordon, but the couple in question are the elderly parents of the owner of this hotel. I can't rightly send them out in the cold."

Tap, tap…"I'm not asking you to do that. I'm simply asking that you give them another room."

"There are no others. I'm sorry."

"No other rooms?" There had to be another room; she had reserved one! "Do you see my children over there, Mr. Green? Mary's only a baby. Would you send her out into the cold?"

He truly did appear remorseful. She brightened her smile and forced her toe to be still.

"Not by choice, no, I wouldn't. But it's out of my hands."

"Whose hands would it be in, then, Mr. Green?" This error would be corrected or she was not Lilleth Preston. "We'll wait right here in the lobby until you find the person who can correct this error."

"It won't do any good. No rooms means no rooms. The hotel is booked up long term. There won't be a room here or anywhere else for a good while." Mr. Green reopened the register and flipped through a few pages. "Look for yourself. There's the Grange meeting in town. All the farmers and their families are here for it."

She would not take the children back out in the cold. They had only now quit shivering.

"Be that as it may, I do have a reservation." Lilleth looked about. There was nothing for it. "We'll take the lobby, then. The chairs by the fire will do well enough for now."

It served Mr. Green right to be choking on his Adam's apple.

"Come along, Jess," she called toward the fireplace. "Let's have a bite to eat before we settle into our chairs for the evening."

"May I be of service in some way?" said a low voice from behind her.

A deep breath, hands planted on her hips and a slow pivot brought her about to face a well-dressed man standing beside Mr. Green.

"And you would be?" She arched a brow. This had better be someone who could fix the situation.

"The owner of this establishment. Is there a problem?" he asked.

"There most certainly is, Mr...." She shooed her hand between them, since he hadn't felt it necessary to reveal his name. "My reservation has been given away. According to Mr. Green, my children and I have no place to go but out in the cold to freeze to death."

"There is the meeting of the Grange. The whole town is booked."

"And I am one of the people who booked."

"I understand your frustration, ma'am. Let me think on it a moment." The hotel owner frowned and twirled his mustache between his thumb and forefinger. "There is Mrs. O'Hara's. She might have a room."

For some reason this made Mr. Green's eyes go wide as dollars.

"Very well, I suppose that will have to do." If it didn't she'd be back to camp out in this lobby. "And where will I find Mrs. O'Hara?"

"A few streets north of here will be a saloon. Make a right and go three blocks. That will take you near the edge of town. You can't miss the place. It's the only building around."

She'd rather not walk the children past a saloon, but there appeared to be no help for it.

She bundled Mary up tight. Jess took the bags.

"Give my regards to Mrs. O'Hara," Mr. Hotel

Owner called as she hustled the children out into the first snowfall of the season.

"Auntie Lilleth," Jess said, his shoulders hunched under the burden of the bags. "I hope Mrs. O'Hara's place isn't far. It's so cold I can't rightly feel my toes."

"Careful, Jess, ears are everywhere."

Trace opened the front door to Clark Clarkly's Private Lending Library, stumbled inside and then closed the door with the heel of his shoe.

He shivered from the chill lingering in his coat and dumped the load of books on his desk, letting them fall out of order. He tossed his broken glasses on the pile.

Ordinarily, he would light a fire in the big hearth that took up most of the wall behind his desk, but not this afternoon. Snow drifted past the window, growing heavier by the minute, and he needed to get to Hanispree Mental Hospital.

Unless he missed his guess, the staff wouldn't venture away from their cozy quarters to make sure the inmates were warm. It was back out into the cold for good old Clarkly.

Over the years, as an investigative journalist for the family paper, Trace had uncovered plenty of nasty secrets. Hanispree Mental Hospital had some of the worst. It was a stink hole of corruption. The more he poked around, the more determined he was to expose the malignant soul of the place.

To the casual observer, Hanispree looked like a resort where the wealthy might come to relax. Its gardens were manicured and the marble staircase inside gleamed. Expensive wood floors reflected layers of polish.

The truth that he had discovered ate at his gut. Polished floors and gleaming marble were a facade. Hanispree Mental Hospital was little more than a prison for the cast-off members of wealthy families. He was certain that some of them had no mental illness whatsoever.

A movement beyond the window caught his attention. He figured he'd be the only one foolhardy enough to go outdoors with a storm blowing in. He walked to the window and pulled aside the filmy curtain.

What the devil? Lilleth and her little brood were making their way down the boardwalk, their bodies leaning into the wind. He'd assumed they would be settled into the hotel by now.

He started to reach for the doorknob, to run after her and find out if there was something amiss.

But she had a husband, no doubt a fine man who was at this moment coming to her aid. Trace would do well to remember that he was not himself at the moment, but Clark Clarkly.

If she discovered who he was it might spell disaster for the exposé he was writing. If his true identity was revealed, what would happen to all the folks at Hanispree? He needed to keep his distance.

Trace peered after Lilleth, his eye to the window-pane trying to see up the street, where Mr. Gordon no doubt waited with open arms.

The investigative journalist in him began to gnaw at something. It was trivial, really. But Lilleth detested being called Lilly. He'd witnessed her wrestling half-grown boys to the ground for teasing her with that name.

A knock low down on the front door brought his attention and his eye away from the window.

He opened the door to let in a flurry of flakes and young Sarah Wilson.

"Little Sarah." He closed the door behind her, then brushed an inch of snowflakes from the brim of her hat. "What are you doing out in this weather?"

"Good day, Mr. Clarkly. I've come to borrow a book."

Bless her heart, coming out in the elements. He was familiar with Sarah. She was a nine-year-old bundle of curiosity, as well as a dedicated reader. Her mother was in frail health, and Sarah escaped into stories as often as she could.

Clark Clarkly and his lending library did have their uses in the community. He wasn't a complete waste.

"As luck would have it, I picked up a shipment of new books just an hour ago." Trace lurched toward the desk and snatched one up, along with his shattered spectacles. "I've just the thing for a girl your age, Miss Sarah."

He opened the ledger on his desk and Sarah signed her name in it, her promise to return the book.

"I'll bring it back real soon," she said.

"Not until the weather clears." He would give her the book to keep, along with a few others, when his assignment was finished and he went back home to Chicago. "Come along, I'll see you home."

Trace put on a heavy coat, picked up his collection of new books and gathered Sarah's mittened hand in his.

Outside, he closed the door behind him and glanced in the direction that Lilleth had gone, but she and her family had vanished.

Met up with her husband, no doubt, the lucky man. In his mind's eye, Trace saw the pair of them snuggled in front of a snapping fire. He wished his Lils and her man the best, truly he did.

"You're going to like this story, little lady." Trace walked in a direction away from Hanispree Mental Hospital, but there was no help for it. "It's the tale of a girl just your age."

Main Street was deserted, the silence profound. Only the shuffle of Lilleth's and Jess's footsteps on the boardwalk disturbed it.

Wisely, the folks of Riverwalk had withdrawn

into their homes. Tendrils of smoke curling out of fireplaces made the cold outside seem that much worse. Only yards away, people were tucked into houses and fully booked hotels, enjoying warmth and companionship.

With any luck, Mrs. O'Hara's place, whether it be a boardinghouse or private home with an extra room—Mr. Hotel Owner hadn't offered that information—would be warm and have food for the children.

Biting cold wasn't the only thing troubling her about Main Street this afternoon. The utter stillness was almost spooky. Out in the open, with no one else about, it seemed that eyes observed her every step. It was silly, of course, as she'd been careful.

A block back, she had been startled by a curtain being drawn aside. Her gasp had nearly woken baby Mary, who slept sweet and warm, against her breast.

"It's all right, Auntie Lilleth," Jess had said. "It's probably Mr. Clarkly. The sign over the door says that place is his lending library."

"It makes sense that Mr. Clarkly would be a librarian, the way he stacked those books in alphabetical order." For some reason it didn't bother her that he might be watching. Funny, when for the last two weeks she'd done nothing but live in fear of folks who stared too intently at her family.

"And Jess, don't forget, call me Mother. Anyone might hear you."

"Uncle Alden won't come to Riverwalk." Jess

shifted the small valise under his left arm to his right. "He's too afraid of ghosts."

True, Alden Hanispree had an unnatural fear of them. It was probably the very thing that had spared her sister's life. Had he not been such a fearful little man he might have murdered Bethany instead of having her committed to his haunted mental hospital.

Still, just because Alden Folger Hanispree was a cowardly man didn't mean that he wasn't dangerous.

Dangerous, and greedy for their inheritance, he was a powerful enemy to her niece and nephew.

"He might send someone, though." Lilleth stopped. She lifted her nephew's chin in her fingers and looked him in the eye. "I'll protect you, I swear it. But Jess, we can't be too careful. Watch every word you say and don't trust anyone but me."

"I wish my father was still alive. Uncle Alden couldn't hurt us then."

"I wish that, too." Lilleth traced the curve of Jess's cold cheek. It had been only six months since his father's death. Too little time to keep Jess's eyes from becoming moist. "But he sees us from heaven, I'm sure of it."

"Do you think, somehow from way up there, he can help us sneak Mama out of the mental hospital?"

"Well, if he can, you know he will, and if not, maybe he'll send someone our way who can help us."

She couldn't imagine who that would be, since she wouldn't allow anyone close enough to be able to help. She wouldn't say so to Jess, but it would be she who would have to figure a way to get Bethany away from Hanispree.

"Everything will turn out fine, Jess, don't you worry." Lilleth shifted the baby in her arms. She was small for a twelve-month-old, but nonetheless the weight was beginning to take a toll on Lilleth's back. "We'd better get to Mrs. O'Hara's before we freeze."

"Sure, Ma." Jess stepped forward with a long stride.

If her brother-in-law was watching from above, as she firmly believed, he would be proud of his only son. Jess was a brave and intelligent boy.

Praise the saints, they were nearly to the saloon, then only a few more blocks to sanctuary.

"Jess, come walk on the far side of me."

Things went on in a saloon that a ten-year-old didn't need to be privy to. It would take a heavier snowfall than this to keep men of low morals and women of loose values from their amusement.

Despite the cold, the front door was open to let out the choking smoke that built up in those places. If it were up to Lilleth, Jess would never be old enough to witness mostly exposed bosoms and the men ogling them.

"When we walk past the front door of the saloon, squeeze your eyes closed."

"Yes, ma'am," he agreed, but a grin crossed his face. And weren't his eyes cracked open a slit?

Well, a grin was better than tears. Blooming adolescence would be something for Bethany to deal with once they set her free.

All would be right when she was Auntie Lilleth again, free to spoil and coddle.

They had taken only a few steps around the corner of saloon when the wind began to howl. Cold air bit through their wool coats. Mary whimpered in her sleep. The three blocks to Mrs. O'Hara's couldn't come soon enough.

It became difficult to see through the swirling snow.

Just in time, Lilleth spotted a house in the distance.

"That way, Jess." She pointed through the shifting white veil.

In another moment a front porch came into view. A front porch with a red lantern hanging from the eves!

It couldn't be. Mr. Hotel Owner would not have sent her here…he couldn't have. Maybe Mrs. O'Hara simply liked red lanterns.

In any case, there was nothing for it but to knock on the door. The children couldn't take much more of the cold. Lilleth's own feet were becoming icy stubs.

The door opened after the third knock. Dim light and warmth spread over the porch.

"Is there something I can do for you, missus? Are you lost? And in this weather!"

Jess didn't bother to hide his grin or squeeze his eyes to respectable slits. Clearly, he was bedazzled by the woman with nearly purple hair, clown-red cheeks and eyes lined with black. Or more likely it was her mostly exposed bosom that made his eyes pop wide in wonder.

"No, not lost." Lilleth took Jess by the shoulder and turned him to face the street. "The owner of the Riverwalk Hotel directed me here after he gave away my room."

Well! Mr. Hotel Owner would not insult both her and Mrs. O'Hara by his little joke. This would not be the last he heard of it.

"On occasion I do rent upstairs rooms. But this wouldn't be the place for you and your children. It wouldn't be seemly. I'm sorry."

"I understand, Mrs. O'Hara. We'll find another place."

"I hope you do. I wouldn't turn you away, but there's the children, you see."

Yes, there were the children. Lilleth hustled Jess down the steps. Mr. Hotel Owner would be well aware of them before this night was through.

Chapter Two

One mile outside of town, Trace opened the gate of Hanispree Mental Hospital and walked through.

Apparently neither Dr. Merlot nor Nurse Goodhew had braved the weather to come outside and lock it for the night. Good luck for Trace—it saved him having to scale the tall stone wall surrounding the place.

The grounds of the hospital looked like a winter playground. The pristine snow covering everything resembled a sparkling blanket. Now that the storm had blown away, the moon shone down to make the area glisten.

But the wind was cold as needles.

To anyone who didn't know better, which would be nearly everyone until he finished his exposé, Hanispree was a lovely place to house the mentally ill. Benches and flowerbeds, bare at this time of year, were connected by a series of winding paths. The building itself was made of the same stone as the wall, with three stories of windows overlooking the elegant park.

To Trace's knowledge, no inmate of the hospital had ever set foot on the paths or sat upon the benches, even when the park was at its loveliest in the spring.

A shiver took him from the inside out. One day soon he would have this place shut down. The patients would be better off away from here, housed in institutions where their well-being was important to the caregivers.

Trace walked across the grounds toward a wide front porch, leaving a trail of footprints in the snow. The verandah, lined end to end with rocking chairs, welcomed him forward.

Through the front window the glow of a fire in the hearth cast golden light into the night. Too bad the aura of comfort was a lie.

Unseen in the dark, he watched through the window for a moment. Nurse Goodhew dozed in a fireside chair with her stocking-clad feet stretched toward the flames.

To call Mrs. Goodhew a nurse was like calling a grade-schooler a professor. From what he had learned, she was there for appearances only. Well, also to keep Dr. Merlot entertained of an evening.

Ah, here came the good doctor now, tiptoeing toward the snoring Mrs. Goodhew and touching her where a gentleman shouldn't.

Spy time was over; if Trace didn't get inside now, he might be shivering on the porch until they finished their tawdry business.

He rapped on the door. When a few moments later Nurse Goodhew opened it, she was wearing her shoes and a sour-looking smile. Dr. Merlot was nowhere to be seen.

"Good evening, Mrs. Goodhew. I've come with a delivery of books." He stepped inside, then stomped the snow from his feet. He took off his hat and thumped it against his thigh.

"Mr. Clarkly! Really, this floor was spotless. Who do you think will clean it now?"

"Why?" Trace lifted his spectacles an inch off his nose and peered at the floor through the broken glass. "I do beg your pardon, Nurse Goodhew. I didn't mean to create a mess."

He shook his head, adding a few more splatters to the floor.

"You must be a madman, coming out in this weather to bring books to people who can't even understand a word on the page."

"Yes, but I'm certain they will enjoy the pictures." He pulled the book on top of the stack from under his arm, opened it and extended it for her to see. "Look, we've got animals of every kind, frolicking in water." He turned the page. "Or nibbling grass."

"Give them here, then." Nurse Goodhew took

the stack. "I'll see them delivered first thing in the morning."

She wouldn't, of course. She never did.

"Thank you. I'm sure your patients will be grateful for your kindness." Trace shook his shoulders, dropping more globs of melting snow on the floor. "Oh my, beg pardon again. If you'll allow me, I'll clean this up before I go. It'll just take an instant."

"See that it does. That water will leave a mark if you're not quick about it."

"To be sure, Mrs. Goodhew."

"I'll be back with cleaning rags." She frowned at him authoritatively. "Don't move from that spot."

"Oh no, not an inch, I swear it."

Half a second after she stepped out of the room, Trace slipped off his boots and coat. He hurried to the desk where the key to the back door of the inmates' cells was kept. The second drawer down, he recalled, under a bottle of whiskey.

Tonight, there was only the bottle of whiskey.

He hurried back, stepped into his boots and put on his coat, and waited two full minutes for the nurse to return with her cleaning rags.

She shoved them at him with another frown. He made quick work of drying the floor. He'd lose some time now, having to figure a new way into the patients' wing.

He walked toward the gate in case anyone was

watching, then followed the brick wall around the back of the building.

His first stop was the woodpile. He shoved his useless glasses in his pocket. He loaded his arms with firewood, then made trip after trip to a window that he knew had a broken latch.

The trouble was, the window was eight feet off the ground. The snow was only a foot high. While scaling something seven feet tall wouldn't be hard, scaling and opening at the same time would be impossible.

The only thing to do was stack the wood under the window, climb the pile, then open the window. After that, he could go in and open the back door and bring the wood in that way, or he could avoid all those steps by tossing the wood through the open window, then climbing in after it. Tossing and climbing would take more effort, but going though the door would take more time.

Since the folks inside were probably shivering, he decided on tossing.

In all it took twenty minutes, but he didn't fear being discovered. Inmate care was more of an afterthought here, especially at night, with only Goodhew and Merlot in attendance. From Trace's experience, they tended to disappear from their shifts between the hours of seven and nine.

It was now seven-ten, giving Trace the time he needed.

He scooped up a load of wood and carried it to old Mrs. Murphy's room. There was a bolt on the outside of the door to insure she did not get out.

He slid it open and stepped into her room.

"Good evening, Mrs. Murphy." The old woman lay on her bed, curled up and shivering under a thin, dirty blanket.

Anger burned hot in him to see her treated so carelessly. Because she was frail and forgetful, her family paid Alden Hanispree a huge amount every month to keep her here. Chances were they were not aware of her meager conditions.

His research had uncovered a miserable truth. Visits by family and friends were by appointment only. An hour before the call the patient would be transferred to a luxurious suite for the duration of the visit. If a few patients did complain to a visitor, well, they were mentally ill. Who would believe their word over a doctor's?

Lies and secrets were the shadows darkening these halls. Soon Trace would have all the evidence he needed and the truth about Hanispree would be told.

Trace lit a fire in the old woman's fireplace, then watched to make sure it burned good and hot.

"Good night, Mrs. Murphy. I'll see you again soon."

The gray head nodded under her cover. "You are

quite considerate for a ghost, young man. I'm sorry
you passed before your time."

He had told her many times that he wasn't a ghost,
but it was just as well that she didn't remember. The
lighting of unexplained fires and the appearance of
extra food were easily blamed on the supernatural.

In under an hour he had brought warmth to every
room but one. That door didn't have a bolt. A heavy
lock made it impossible to get inside.

The investigator in him wanted to know what
was in there. He'd heard stories of other institutions
where the inmates were actually tortured in the name
of research. One of these days he'd find a way into
that second-story room.

Having done everything he could for the inmates,
he went outside. He stepped beside his own footprints going away, thinking that it was a good thing
for the old ghost stories. A spirit would be credited
with all manner of strange happenings.

Had she not been homeless, freezing and responsible for two children, Lilleth would feel quite pleased.

Dinner at the hotel could not have gone better. In
the end they had been kicked out of the restaurant,
but she and the children had caused a bucketload
of complaints to be served up to Mr. Hotel Owner.

Mary, having been confined to Lilleth's arms for
much of the day, wanted to crawl about on the floor.

She wailed and carried on because she was not allowed to do so.

Jess accidentally spilled his milk on the tablecloth three times. Naturally, Lilleth had insisted on fresh linen with each accident.

And, by the saints, why could the kitchen not prepare her steak correctly? The waiter had to return it several times before it was cooked just so.

As annoyed as the other patrons were at her little family, they were aghast when the owner, with his own hands, escorted them out into the elements with orders not to return. Surely the fellow deserved every frown cast his way.

But what to do now? It was not that Lilleth couldn't afford a room, there simply were none to be had. Perhaps the livery would have a stall, but wouldn't that cause a stir? It might be fodder for gossip from one end of town to another. Poor frazzled mother of two, denied rooms at both the hotel and the brothel, ending up in a pile of straw?

She had slept in worse places than a clean pile of straw before, but she couldn't afford the attention that it would draw to her. She needed to remain in the shadows.

Oh, dear, she should have considered that during dinner.

While delivering Mr. Hotel Owner his just rewards had been deeply satisfying, the little show had drawn the attention of every diner in the hotel restaurant. She would have to be more discreet in the future.

"At least the snow has quit," Jess said, fitting his sister into the curve of his elbow.

The poor little thing continued to squirm and fuss. She hadn't been out of her or Jess's arms in ever so long.

Pain cramped Lilleth's fingers. They felt like frozen claws clutching the handles of the valises. "That's a mercy, but the wind! Make sure to keep the blanket over Mary's head."

"She keeps pulling it off."

It wouldn't take long for her tiny ears to freeze, even covered by a hat. They needed shelter and they needed it now. The dark and the cold were swiftly becoming mortal enemies.

A church, then. Perhaps they would find sanctuary there, if only for this night. Lilleth scanned the rooftops of town, looking for a steeple. Where could it be?

Every town had a church! Hopefully, she'd find one with someone in attendance.

"Look there." Jess pointed down the street. "There's a lamp on in Mr. Clarkly's library."

"Hurry, Jess, we've got to get there before he puts it out and turns in for the night."

Doing so took longer than she dreamed it would. The boardwalk had grown icy. Jess half slipped a dozen times. In the end, she abandoned the valises in front of Horton File's Real Estate, Homes for Sale or Rent. She took Mary from Jess's arms and steadied him.

"The lamp's just gone off!" Her brave young nephew sounded truly alarmed.

"We're nearly there. He'll hear us when we knock."

She prayed that he wouldn't turn them away. For all that he was a stranger, Mr. Clarkly seemed a decent fellow.

It took forever, but at last they stood in front of the door of Clark Clarkly's Private Library.

Lilleth knocked. Stabbing pain shot through her frozen hand. She bit her lip to hold in the agony and keep the tears out of her eyes.

Footsteps sounded inside, coming toward the door. Lilleth would simply faint into his arms if he attempted to turn them away, and it might not be an act.

The door opened.

"Mrs. Gordon!" Mr. Clarkly gaped at her without his spectacles on. Even in her desperation, she noticed that he had uncommonly appealing eyes, blue with green flecks. Bless the man for a saint, those eyes reflected more than a bit of concern.

He reached for Mary and tucked her in the crook of his arm. With his free hand he touched Lilleth's shoulder and drew her inside.

"Come in, young man," he said to Jess. "You look frozen through."

"I'll just go back," Jess said with chattering teeth, "f-for th-the bags."

"Well now, that won't do." Mr. Clarkly poked his head out the door and peered at the bags lying on the boardwalk a block down. "They'll be safe enough until I get a fire going. Here, take your sister and sit on that chair. There's a book beside it on the table. That should keep her distracted until she's warmed through."

Clark Clarkly knelt beside the fireplace, urging a small flame to life. He performed the chore quickly. His shoulders flexed and contracted under his shirt with his brisk movements.

Praise everything good that the man built a fire with more skill than he displayed walking.

He stood up after a moment, seeming taller than she remembered, straighter of form.

"Thank you, Mr. Clarkly." That simple phrase didn't begin to express her gratitude. "I can't think of what might have happened if—"

"No thanks needed, Mrs. Gordon." He took her cold hands in his big warm ones for an instant while he led her toward a chair by the fire. "Sit tight while I fetch your bags."

Mr. Clarkly hurried out the door and closed it behind him before the wind could sweep away the warmth beginning to hug the room.

His gait had been quick, efficient. Judging by his swift return, he hadn't taken a single tumble while he was fetching the bags.

He dropped them on the floor, and then instantly forgot he had put them there. His first step forward brought him stumbling across the room, where he careened off his desk and landed at her feet, with one hand caught in her skirt.

"So sorry…I beg your pardon. My glasses." He glanced about, blinking hard. "Blind as a bat without them."

"Mr. Clarkly." She untangled his hand where it gripped her ankle through her skirt. "I am the one indebted to you."

One could almost wish, however unkind it might be, that he wouldn't find his glasses. He had eyes a woman could look into and get lost.

Silly, Lilleth, silly, she chided herself. Getting lost in a man's eyes. What nonsense!

Clark Clarkly had come to her aid and nothing more.

Still, it was disappointing to see him find his broken spectacles. He frowned at them, tossed them aside and rooted through a desk drawer until he found another pair.

The man did need to see, after all. She'd be a silly goose to believe that staring into a man's eyes would result in anything more than heartache, even if he did seem uncommonly kind.

Relief eased the iciness from her bones as much as the flames did.

Mr. Clarkly sat on the floor, playing with Mary and speaking to Jess in low tones. The fire crackled, sounding like music in the cozy library. A teakettle in another room began to whistle.

What she wouldn't give to be able to sing the rest of the tension from her body. But no, that might not be wise. The chances were slim, but her voice might be recognized.

But humming, now that would be a comfort. Anyone could hum and sound the same. So she did. She hummed her favorite tune, one that had comforted her since she was a little girl.

For some reason, that made Mr. Clarkly quit talking to Jess and stare at her with the most peculiar expression on his face.

There was something almost…but not quite, familiar about it. Well, that was silly. She'd never met Mr. Clarkly until today.

"This ought to warm you." Trace grazed Lilleth's hand, passing her a cup of steaming tea.

He didn't think her fingers looked as blue as they had.

What wouldn't he give to be the man with the right to hold them to his heart and warm them thoroughly.

After half an hour beside the fire she had only now quit shivering.

Her husband couldn't be worth much, allowing his family to become wandering icicles.

"I can't think of how to thank you, Mr. Clarkly." She closed her fingers about the teacup and shut her eyes for an instant. "I thought I'd never be warm again."

Trace crouched beside her chair. He had a mind to stroke the ringlets that strayed from under her hat. He'd give up a lot to be able to loop his thumb through one of those red curls, to touch it in the familiar way a man would touch his woman's hair.

In any event, she wasn't his woman. Even if she were free, he wouldn't risk his assignment by revealing his identity. He couldn't. The patients at Hanispree depended on him.

His family was counting on him to deliver an exposé by the New Year. Being employed by one's parents added extra pressure to deliver. Not only that, there was sibling rivalry to be taken into account.

All his brothers and his sister worked for the *Chicago Gazette*. Although, since his sister had become a mother, she had quit the investigative side of the business. On occasion the job became dangerous.

That was one of the reasons that the Ballentines sometimes worked in disguise.

The other reason was that several of their investigations were sufficiently well known that the Ballentines were often recognized. When a case involved secrecy, as this one did, a disguise was called for.

He had picked Clarkly because the character was as unlike his real self as could be. No one could possibly recognize him.

It wasn't easy living in the skin of someone who wasn't real. It was lonely, not being able to let anyone close.

Still, his job was deeply rewarding and made the temporary isolation worthwhile. Over the years his investigations had improved the lots of many people. They'd put swindlers out of business and criminals behind bars.

He couldn't imagine doing anything else for a living.

Trace watched Lilleth sipping from the teacup. He'd always found her mouth to be pretty, but now, as a woman full grown, her lips were a man's fantasy. Moist with hot tea, they glistened in the glow of the fire.

"Mrs. Gordon." Crouched down as he was, his eyes met hers over the rim of the cup. Her mouth stilled over a porcelain rose. "There's something troubling me. I hope you don't consider this forward of me to ask, but Mr. Gordon…oughtn't he be—"

Her pretty lips puckered, as though they had tasted something sour…or needed to be kissed.

For the hundredth time since he had run Lilleth down at the train station, he cursed the decision to become Clarkly. He ought to have adopted his favorite identity, Johnny Kaid, fastest cowboy with a rope or a gun.

Curse it! Johnny was daring, but Clark was safer, and safe was all-important at this moment.

"Here? By my side, you mean?" Lilleth set the cup on her lap and stared down at it. "My husband ran off. I don't know where he is."

"It was nearly a year back," Jess said, hugging his sister close. "Mary was only a newborn."

Poor, brave Lils! On her own with two young children.

"I can't tell you how sorry I am." He couldn't help it; he reached over and held her fingers where they gripped the cup.

"No need to fret, Mr. Clarkly." Lilleth shrugged. She sighed and looked into his eyes. "It's been a while now, and to tell you the truth, my husband was a worldly man. In many ways life is easier without him."

"Pa liked his spirits." Jess covered Mary's ears. "More than most."

Trace's world bucked and shifted beneath him. Having Lilleth within touching distance had been temptation enough, with a loving husband standing between them. Without him things had become complicated.

He let go of Lilleth's hands. The man was gone, and no good, but that didn't make her any less legally wed.

"If I can help you, all you need to do is ask."

"You've been kindness itself already. You did no less than save our lives tonight." She set the cup aside. "Please, won't you call me Lilly."

He forced a smile when he wanted to frown. She hated that name. What had happened to make her use it?

"I'd be pleased if you would call me Clark." He pursed his lips, about to offer something improper, given that she was someone else's wife. But he couldn't see any help for it. "I've a room upstairs. I'd be pleased if you and the children would sleep there tonight."

She took off her hat. Whorls and curls reflecting the fire's glow broke free of a bun that would never be able to confine them.

"You are our very own angel, Clark, sent straight down from heaven."

That comment evidently pleased young Jess. He suddenly grinned so widely that the freckles on his cheeks appeared to dance.

Trace was no angel. Not by a yard. An angel wouldn't be glad that her worthless husband had run away.

A heavenly being wouldn't fidget in his chair all through this long, blustery night, wondering if the

virtueless rogue was dead so that he could kiss his
wife. A woman he had no business kissing even if
she were free.

Chapter Three

"Say your prayers, Jess." Lilleth listened to the wind whistle around the dormers of the tidy upstairs bedroom. Mary and Jess lay side by side in a cozy-looking feather bed that Mr. Clarkly had put fresh linens on before retiring downstairs to sleep, presumably, in a chair. "And don't forget to mention Mr. Clarkly."

"Do you think my pa might have sent him to us?"

"Who's to know? I can't say that he didn't." To see the children safe and snug did seem a miracle. If it hadn't been for Mr. Clarkly's generosity—well, that outcome didn't bear thinking of.

She hadn't had a reason to be truly grateful to a man since she could remember. Not since she was a little girl and believed that princes, knights and cowboys rode to the aid of ladies in need.

In those days she'd had a hero. He was her champion and she'd seen her future in his smile. They'd been as close as berries on a vine the summer that she was twelve years old.

She had loved him with all her young heart, and he must have loved her as well, for he had defended her against a pair of bullies and become seriously injured. Then, to her everlasting horror, before his wounds had begun to mend, her mother had shattered her world.

In the dead of night, she had woken Lilleth and Bethany, packed them up and moved three states away to be with the latest in a constant string of inappropriate beaux.

It wasn't that her mother was a whore in the normal sense, as her reputation suggested. It was more that she was needy. She let men take care of her in exchange for her affections. Unfortunately for Lilleth and Bethany, their mother's affections latched on to the wrong sorts of men.

As little girls they had become skilled, yes, even creative, at keeping one step ahead of groping male hands. Because of Bethany, what might have been a harrowing lot became a game. Lilleth's older sister never let her feel less of herself because of the behavior of men. Together, they practiced ducking, dodging, stomping and pinching. At night they would whisper in bed, recounting tales of near escape and retaliation. Some girls might have withered under such an upbringing, but she and Bethany dodged and ducked through it all.

But life was what it was. Lilleth had been formed by it and so had her sister. Bethany escaped into marriage, while Lilleth took her voice on the road with a traveling show.

Since Bethany loved her husband and Lilleth loved to sing, it had all turned out well enough.

Until six months ago, that is, when Bethany's husband had died suddenly of a fever.

Lilleth kissed Jess good-night and stroked the curly hair at Mary's temple. Her nephew would be a good man. Bethany would raise him to be like his father.

"Uncle Alden can't get to us here. Mr. Clarkly is downstairs." Jess yawned and turned on his side, facing the blaze that Clark had laid in the small upstairs fireplace. "We'll get Mama out of that place, just see if we don't."

"We will, I promise we will," Lilleth said. Firelight cast shadows on Jess's face, making him look like a miniature of his father, Hamilton.

How Alden and Hamilton could be twins was a mind-twisting mystery. Hamilton, older by a few moments, had been a good man, as honorable as he was handsome. Alden was a nervous little fellow who, unless surrounded by a group of fawning minions, was frightened of his shadow. And of ghosts…especially ghosts.

It was understandable that the wealthy Hanisprees, upon their deaths, had willed Alden a monthly allowance and Hamilton their entire fortune.

For a man as greedy as Alden, an allowance was not nearly enough. He coveted his brother's inheritance, which now belonged to Bethany.

Lilleth was certain that, had he not been petrified that she would haunt him, Alden would have killed Bethany to take control of the fortune. But now, having incarcerated Bethany, all he need do was control her children.

That he would never do. Lilleth vowed it on her life. Why, she would tear him to shreds with her bare hands if he got within arm's reach of them.

All at once the wind stopped and snow swept past the dormer window, silent and beautiful. She took a cleansing breath to banish Alden from her mind.

She walked to the window, unbuttoning the bodice of her gown and watching snowflakes sailing past. Sometimes when she was stressed she would try to bring her childhood hero's face to mind. But time had blurred his image; she couldn't see him anymore.

It didn't matter, really. He would have changed a great deal. Even if she ran into him on the street he'd be altered beyond recognition, and so would she.

Yes, life was what it was. All those years ago she had cried for weeks, before tucking Trace Ballentine into a precious corner of her heart.

Aside from her brother-in-law, Trace had been

the only bone-deep good man—boy, really—that she had ever met.

Until Clark Clarkly, that is. So far he seemed to be quite decent.

The poor man didn't know he was sheltering a criminal. For his own good, she would have to be out of his house as soon as she could get her bearings. Hopefully, tomorrow morning.

Lilleth Preston didn't like being on the wrong side of the law. She was a singer, a sister and an auntie. Three things that she adored and had built her life around.

Curse Alden Hanispree for forcing her to kidnap her sister's children.

It was late. On any other night Trace would have been asleep hours before. Early to bed and early to rise and all that. But Lilleth was upstairs, abandoned and unprotected.

He lurched out of his chair for the tenth time in under an hour to pace before the dying fire. The fact that she was, for all accounts, unmarried was a torment and a temptation, but he would deal with that.

Unprotected! Now that was a problem more difficult to cope with.

Yes, she had grown to be a capable and resilient woman.

And no, he was no more able to leave her to the

whims of fate now than he had been when she was a child.

"Well hell, Lils," he muttered. "What am I supposed to do?"

He stomped to the front door and snatched it open. Icy air bit his nose and chilled his ears. It did not, however, do much in the way of clearing his head.

He couldn't give her safe harbor without compromising the secrecy of his mission. He couldn't send her and the children out into the elements.

He could try to get some sleep. Occasionally, the answers to perplexing problems came to him while he slumbered. More than a few puzzles had knit together in his dreams.

He closed the front door, shook off a shiver and tried once again to fold his body in a too-small chair.

Knees up, shoulders hunched, neck twisted, with eyes closed and sheep counted…this time he would make it work.

"Stars shine bright, sleep tight tonight," he whispered. His eyes popped wide-open.

From what dusty part of his brain had he remembered that? Years ago it had been Lilleth's nightly farewell when, far past the time when most girls were allowed out, she would peck his cheek and dash through the trees toward home.

"Stars shine bright, sleep tight tonight," he repeated, dusting off the phrase and polishing it. Amazingly, he began to get sleepy.

Behind his eyelids he saw young Lilleth in the woods.

Summer heat shimmered off the ground even though it was hours after sundown. Leaves on the trees drooped, looking wilted under the light of a full moon.

She ran toward Red Leaf Pond holding the hem of her white nightgown in her fists.

She didn't appear to see him sitting on the rotting tree trunk at the edge of the pond. She must have been trying to escape the heat, just as he was.

His own ma and pa didn't mind their boys running loose after dark. His sister complained to high heaven, but she was a girl, and therefore confined to the safety of home.

But Lilleth didn't live by those rules. Her mother wouldn't care that she was out, even if she knew.

Just now, Lils ran barefoot and free. Her red hair streamed out behind her, winking at the moon.

At the water's edge she waded in past her ankles, then began to lift her shift, clearly intending to draw the thin, worn fabric over her head.

"Hey, Lils!" He stood up quickly and strode into the moonlight. "Mind if I come in, too?"

She dropped the hem of her nightgown and grinned at him. "I'll race you to the middle," she called.

She waited for him to strip to his underdrawers

before she dived in. She didn't need a head start, for she swam like a tadpole.

They met in the center, circling around each other and laughing. Moonlight dappled the surface of the pond where they kicked and splashed.

"Oh." Lilleth ducked under the water, then surfaced again. "The day's been blistering. This feels so good."

"Yeah, but Lils, you shouldn't be out by yourself at night. It's not safe."

"Safer than home, I guess." She brushed her hand across her face, sluicing water from her eyes and nose. "Mama has a new man and Beth and I haven't got him figured out yet. Besides, I'm not alone, you're here."

"I might not have been." He ducked under the water and came up blowing out a mouthful, pretending to be the spout of a fancy fountain. "What if Horn and Pard Higgins are slinking about?"

"Well, they aren't. And you *are* here."

With that she flipped beneath the water and grabbed hold of his feet. She yanked him under. He caught her around the middle, feeling ribs under cotton, and then hoisted her up. He surfaced in time to see her flying through the air, laughing and sputtering.

They played like that for a long time before Lils began to shiver and they swam for shore.

He put his clothes on while she wrung out her hair.

"I'll walk you home," he said.

"I'm going to run." She flashed him a grin with pond water still speckling her lashes. "You won't be able to catch up."

"My legs are longer."

"Mine are quicker." She bounced up on her toes and pecked his cheek. "Stars shine bright, sleep tight tonight."

Then she was off, a streak in the moonlight. He laughed out loud. His longer legs never were a match for her quicker ones, but at least he'd get there in time to see her close her front door safely behind her.

Trace twitched in his sleep. He groaned and woke up.

That night, he never did see Lils open her door. He heard her scream.

Bursting out of the woods, he saw the Higgins boys push Lilleth to the ground. Horn knelt over her, pinning her wrists to the parched earth. Pard laughed and called her obscene names.

Lils spat back oaths that would have sent ordinary mischief-makers running, but Pard and Horn weren't ordinary. The twins fed off each other, one disrespectful and the other mean. Even adults kept out of their way.

Running full speed, Trace plowed into Horn, but didn't see the jagged stick that Lils had gripped in her fist, ready to jab her assailant with.

He knocked Horn over. The bully slammed into his brother. Blood spurted, some from Horn's ear and some from Pard's nose.

It looked as if the boys didn't care for having their own blood spilled, because they ran away crying and cursing. And a good thing, too, because Trace couldn't have moved a muscle to protect Lilleth.

The stick that she had intended to jab Horn with now stuck out of his own chest. Blood pulsed from a long gash across his ribs. Lils looked like a blur leaning over him, pressing his wound and yelling at him. After a moment even her screams sounded like whispers.

Trace sat up in his chair and let his feet hit the cold floor. He'd been sick—close to death, he'd been told. Mostly, all he remembered was a visit from Lils.

She had come to his house weeping, and blowing a kiss at his scar. He told her he didn't mind it, that the scar was bound to heal into an *L*, for Lils. She'd laughed and dried her tears.

That's when she gave him a quick, sweet kiss on the lips, pressed his hand to her heart and vowed to marry him and only him.

Then, suddenly, she was gone, and no one knew where or even exactly when her mother had packed them off.

He'd been right about the scar. From that day until now, all he'd had of Lilleth was her initial across his heart.

* * *

Lilleth stepped cautiously onto the boardwalk. Ice crunched under her feet. Early morning sunshine peeked under her hat and gave the illusion of warmth even though her breath fogged in front of her face.

The storm had blown away with the dawn, and so had some of her worries. She couldn't help it; she had to sing, if only under her breath.

Horton File, Realtor, had been the most agreeable of men. But then, who wouldn't have been, receiving such an excessive amount of money to rent the only vacant house in Riverwalk?

Lilleth felt agreeable as well, even though she had been all but fleeced. She and the children had a place to live. A place that Mr. File had assured her was a lovely, furnished cabin tucked into the woods only steps from town.

The privacy of a cabin hidden among the trees was more than she had hoped for. The rent wouldn't be a problem for the brief time they would live in Riverwalk. With luck, it would be only a month, maybe less, just until she figured out a way to free Bethany.

With sunshine smiling upon the town, Riverwalk appeared to be a charming place. Like many communities in South Dakota it was growing fast, filling with families and their commerce. Between the Realtor's office and Clark's lending library she had passed a dress shop, a barber and a baker.

It was only a couple of hours past sunrise and already the sign on the bakery door read Open for Business.

Clean morning air nipped her cheeks and filled her lungs. Lilly Gordon thoroughly enjoyed the quiet hours just after sunrise.

Lilleth Preston had performed her songs late into the night. Mornings typically found her with her head buried beneath her pillow.

She would miss seeing the sunrise once she returned to her life with Dunbar's Touring Troupe.

Even more, she suspected she would miss the first fresh pastries of the day. She opened the door to Martha's Baked Goods and was greeted by the aromas of cinnamon, vanilla and yeast.

She purchased four cinnamon buns drizzled with honey. The children would be thrilled with the treat.

Bethany would have provided her children with a healthy breakfast of eggs and milk.

But Lilleth wasn't a mother, just an indulgent auntie who had never learned to cook. Life on the road, living from hotel to hotel with a group of traveling performers had never presented her the opportunity to learn.

Well, then, that would be one of her goals this month. By the time they rescued Bethany, the children would be eating meals that she had prepared with her own hands.

Lilleth warmed her fingers about the bag of baked

goods and hurried the three doors down to Clark's place, slipping, sliding and wobbling.

Clark had started a fire while she had been out. Warmth wrapped around her as soon as she stepped inside. Upstairs, she heard Jess's footsteps and Mary's good-morning coos.

Clark sat at his desk, head down on folded arms and fast asleep with a pair of glasses clutched in his fist. The poor man must be exhausted. He couldn't have done more than doze in a chair all night.

"Clark," she whispered. The familiarity of using his first name felt a little awkward, and a lot nice. "I've brought breakfast."

He didn't wake up, but his mouth lifted, revealing the barest hint of a dimple at one corner. My goodness, the man was appealing.

There was something about him that didn't quite make sense. He was a complete bumbler, as likely to trip over his own feet as walk a steady line. Once in a while, though, he wasn't.

Lilleth bent over to peer more closely at his face. She shouldn't; he was nearly a stranger. She leaned another inch toward him. Something about him called to her. Why didn't he seem like a stranger?

She had spent the night in his bed. That must be the reason.

He appeared to be dreaming. She watched his eyes move behind his lids. His lips compressed, then relaxed. Thick dark lashes twitched…they blinked.

Sleep-misted eyes opened wide and blue, then blinked again.

"Good morning, Lilly."

By heavens, there was a dimple. And could she be any more of a ninny, staring and blinking back?

She straightened and backed up, holding the bag of cinnamon rolls between them. "I've brought breakfast."

"Martha's?" He rolled one shoulder, then the other, stretched...grinned and sat up. "I'm starved."

An apology would have been called for, could she have found one appropriate to the situation. But just then Jess came downstairs with Mary in his arms.

"Morning, Ma, Mr. Clarkly. Is that sweets?" His eyes grew wide in anticipation. There were some things that Bethany would have to set straight later on. Her children's diet being the first. "I'm starved."

"Sit down there on the rug in front of the fire," Lilleth told him. Jess did so, placing himself between the hearth and his baby sister. "Careful with the crumbs."

Lilleth sat on the rug and broke off small pieces of cinnamon bun, feeding them to Mary. Clark, with his glasses perched low on his nose, completed the circle. He sat beside her with his ankles crossed and his knees sticking out. He didn't seem to notice that his left knee bumped into her right one.

Any other man would get a swift boot in the...

But this was Clark, and chances were he was oblivious to where his limbs ended up.

"I have good news," Lilleth announced, scooting beyond reach of Clark's knee. "I've found us a place to live!"

"Why, that's… Well, it's…" For some reason it took an instant for his smile to reach his eyes. "Truly wonderful news. Where?"

"We'll be neighbors, Clark. I've rented the cabin in the woods, just down the path behind the lending library."

He choked on cinnamon and honey.

"That's just…" He managed to catch his breath despite the crumbs still lodged in his throat. "I'm pleased as can be."

But he wasn't. And that was as *clear* as could be.

Trace stood on his back porch watching Lilleth and her brood, valises in hand, walking down the path that led into the woods. Cold sunshine winked on the snow and glinted off his fake glasses. He'd have to keep them on, though, even though the glare was making his eyes sting.

At the tree line, Lilleth turned and waved. The confident smile on her face wouldn't last long. In another five minutes she would discover that her cozy, furnished cabin was barely fit to live in.

Trace waved back, but watching while she vanished among the trees made him feel off-kilter. As if something precious had been given, and then snatched away before he'd even had time to blink at the wonder of it.

Trace was a man grounded in reality. Facts were what he lived and breathed.

Still, it couldn't have been an accident that his long-lost Lils had spent the night under his roof. It couldn't have been pure chance that put them both on the same train platform at the same instant in time.

Letting her walk away now felt like an act against their common destiny.

Or could it be that their destinies weren't common? Maybe letting her walk away was fulfilling that.

It was all just a bunch of fancy thinking, anyway, fate and destiny.

Facts, on the other hand, were what they were, no guessing or wondering involved. It would serve him well to keep them in mind.

Here was a hard and cold fact: Lils was walking into a bad situation and taking her children with her.

Another fact was that Trace was honor-bound to protect the inmates at Hanispree, and the safest way to do that was to let Lilleth take that path into the woods and deal with her problems on her own.

And the last fact on his mental list…he would not do it.

Trace picked up the ax leaning against the woodpile beside his back door and followed Lilleth's footprints into the woods.

He grinned, considering a fact he had just added to his mental list. It didn't have a thing to do with fancy thinking; it was as hard as facts go.

Clark Clarkly was going to kiss Lilly Gordon.

Chapter Four

A ray of sunshine filtering through bare tree branches dappled fingers of light on the roof of the small cabin. Close by, Lilleth heard the welcome rush of a creek.

In the event that the cabin did not have an indoor pump, it would be an easy task to fetch water.

"What do you think, Jess?" Lilleth went up the stairs with Mary in her arms. The third step cracked under her weight. "Be careful, this one might need to be replaced."

The broken step was a minor problem, but for the rent she was paying she would make sure the landlord had it repaired by this afternoon.

"The place seems safe, Auntie Lilleth, way back here in the woods." He grinned up at her. "Maybe I can explore later."

Looking safe and being safe weren't necessarily the same thing, but the boy needed to be out, running and playing. Poor Jess had been confined to trains and secrecy for much too long.

"Let's settle in now, and we can explore together."

"You like to climb trees and stuff, Auntie Lils?"

"Let me tell you, when I was your age, you couldn't keep me out of a tree." Not that anyone had ever tried to. "I suppose I can still manage."

Blazes, if she wouldn't make this time as easy on the children as she could. Hiding out in the little cabin for a month might be made into an adventure.

She turned the key in the lock and opened the door.

The very fingers of sunshine that dappled the roof dappled a broken kitchen table. It shone on a floor with layers of dusty things scattered about. It filtered over a lumpy bed where a family of raccoons was suddenly startled from sleep.

Mary squirmed and reached for the floor, but there was not an inch of space that was clean enough to set her down.

"Take Mary outside, will you?" *Tap, tap, tap.* Lilleth fought the urge to kick a crushed pail that she had come close to tripping over. It was best to get the children outdoors for a moment. It wouldn't begin their cabin adventure well to see Auntie in a fit of despair.

"Stay close by," she called after Jess.

He, at least, seemed happy enough, galloping

around to the back of the house with his sister giggling in his arms.

But what was Lilleth going to do? Dusty spiderwebs sagged across shredded curtains at the windows—which, by God's own grace, were at least not broken. The bed was not fit for the raccoons that had just scurried into a back room.

There was a nice stone fireplace, if one ignored the giant mound of ashes spilling out of the hearth. Hours of scrubbing from now, it might be cozy with a couple of chairs set before it.

Naturally, there were no chairs.

No chairs, no indoor pump, not a decent bed. There was the dining table, but one would have to sit on the disgusting floor to make use of it.

And thanks to the family of raccoons, the place smelled. No doubt it also had fleas.

She gathered the hem of her skirt into the crook of her arm.

"We're going to the creek, Auntie Lilleth," Jess called through a cracked board in the wall. "It's real close by."

That was a mercy. It would take endless buckets of hot water to make the place decent enough even to put Mary down.

"Blasted raccoons." Lilleth would start by getting rid of them. "You better have found an escape hole back there. I'm coming in!"

She'd need a weapon, though. There! In the corner

of what used to be the kitchen area, beside a rusted cookstove, was a broom. Too bad no one had ever seen fit too use it.

She held it before her, business end first, and entered the back room with a sweeping motion.

Sure enough, there was a hole. She made contact with a striped tail just as the tip squeezed through.

This apparently was a storage room, stacked from ceiling to floor with buckets, rugs, dishes, more broken furniture and some things she could not identify.

Horton File might believe that this trash counted as furnishings, but he was about to discover that their opinions on what was livable lay miles apart.

Before that, though, she would have to strap Mary to her back in order to clean a spot big enough to set her down.

A faded red blanket lay on the floor. Lilleth picked it up, sneezed, then wadded it up and stuck it in the raccoon hole. She dusted her hands.

If only the cabin didn't smell like old things and wild animal fur.

Night, along with temperatures below freezing, would be here too soon. She would need to clean the fireplace first thing. Then have Jess gather wood.

"Dear Lord, how will I get it all done?" she murmured. Already, grime caked her skin and she hadn't even begun.

The first thing she would need was light, then fire. She walked to the window and yanked on the curtain, which dropped on the floor. Dust billowed out of it and sent her into a full sneezing fit.

She rubbed the window with the hem of her petticoat. A small clear circle appeared on the glass.

Within that circle appeared a man. Clark Clarkly was striding forward with an ax gripped in his fist.

Clark Clarkly was not a bumbler. Well, he was, but not always. Not now. For the past thirty minutes Lilleth had been peeking at him through the window while she passed back and forth, sweeping the floor.

He stood by a woodpile, one stacked from fallen limbs that he had dragged out of the woods. Through the open cabin door she listened to the steady blows of his ax.

As far as she could tell he hadn't come close to chopping off his foot, even though the pile of cut logs now stood thigh high.

One time, when he looked up to see her watching him, he stumbled backward and dropped the ax.

What a puzzle he was. One moment falling all over himself, and the next, as capable a man as she'd ever met.

One would expect a bookish man, one who stacked volumes in alphabetical order, to be fragile in his bearing. Not so Clark. Trip and stumble as he might, beneath those clothes she suspected he was muscle upon muscle. How could he not be, the way he swung his ax.

Passing the window once more, she paused. He didn't notice her this time. She watched the ax circle in the air, then hit a log, splitting it down the center. Clark tossed it aside and spilt another, then another, in the same way.

Those were not the shoulders of a slightly built man. They flexed beneath his shirt with a regular rhythm. Even in the cold, sweat dampened his shirt between his shoulder blades.

To add to his mystery, he was a take-charge kind of individual. One would expect a librarian to be comfortable in the sanctuary of his library, his life as predictable as the next printed page.

But Clark, as soon as he'd glanced about at the rubble-strewn cabin, had taken control of the undertaking. He'd sent the children back to his place, putting Jess in charge of lending out books for the day.

Now here he was, getting her cabin tidy and shipshape. Later she was to come back to his place and spend another night tucked safe under his roof, and no arguments about it.

Truly, she wouldn't tell him no even if she had a choice. There was something about Mr. Clark Clarkly that drew her to him, and it wasn't just a common love of books.

Clark looked up and spotted her at the window. He grinned, wiped one sleeve across his forehead, then waved the ax at her in greeting.

To all appearances, he liked nothing more than to cut and stack wood. Any other man she had known would want something in return for his kindness— which in her mind didn't make it a kindness in the end—but so far Clark hadn't made an improper move toward her.

Still, hadn't it been only a day since he'd snatched her off the boardwalk? She'd known men who hid their true natures much longer.

The light streaming in through the window and the front door suddenly dimmed when the sun passed below the tree line. Time to quit trying to figure out Mr. Clark Clarkly. Whatever tugged at her about him would have to wait.

There was enough work here to keep her busy for a week, and at some point she needed to figure a way to make a secret visit to her sister.

Bethany must be frantic with worry over the children. She had no way of knowing that Lilleth had kidnapped them from their unsavory uncle.

"All finished out here." Clark strode through the door, carrying a load of wood in one arm. Just inside, he stopped abruptly, set the load on the hearth and touched his face. He rooted through his shirt pocket. "Must have lost my glasses someplace."

"I'll help you look." She leaned the broom on the fireplace. "They're probably near the woodpile."

She walked toward the front door, but he stopped her with a hand to her elbow.

"No need to bother, Lilly. It's easier to work blind than have the things slipping off my nose, anyway." He let go of her. "What's next?"

"I'm going to scrub the floor, and you have done enough." Clark looked like a different man without his glasses. It wasn't only his face that seemed different, it was the way he moved. "Go home, Clark. I've taken up way too much of your time."

"A librarian finds himself with an excess of time on occasion." He shuddered and glanced about the cabin. "This is a nightmare for just one person. I'll take care of the holes in the roof."

"You don't have to, really. You've done too much." That was the polite thing to say, and having said it, she hoped that he wouldn't leave.

He took her shoulders in his hands and looked her square in the eye. No doubt this was where he would seek repayment of his kindness.

"I don't have a single thing to do that's more important than helping you, Lilly." He let go of her suddenly, rooted through his pants pocket and pulled out his glasses. "Imagine that! They were there the whole time."

He spun about, crossed the room and stood in the open doorway, with afternoon shadows outlining his silhouette.

"I'm going to stay and help, because that's what

decent folks do." When he turned she thought he
might trip on the threshold, but he didn't.

So far, Clark Clarkly was not like any other man
she had ever known.

Walking up the path toward the cabin, Trace
watched moonlight twinkle in icicles hanging from
the eaves. The day had warmed, but tonight the temperature was dropping in a hurry.

He hoped the cabin was as warm inside as the
firelight shining out of the newly cleaned windows
indicated.

Lilleth had swept, scrubbed and polished herself
to exhaustion. In a few more days the place might
be habitable.

He opened the door and stepped inside.

Lilleth, facing the rusty stove, spun about. Alarm
flashed in her eyes. She clutched the soapy dishrag
that she had been using on the stove to her bosom.

"My word, Clark. You startled me."

Maybe, but that fleeting fear in her expression
seemed more than startled. Maybe she was afraid
that her husband might have suddenly returned. If
the expression on her face was anything to go by, he
could be worse than she or her son had let on.

"I should have knocked." Clark glanced around
the cabin in surprise.

In the few hours that he had been gone she had
accomplished quite a bit. Six chairs, two of which

were placed before the fire, had been wiped clean of the layers of grime that had caked them.

The crate of dishes that he had dragged from the back room earlier were now scrubbed and drying on the table which he had repaired. He wouldn't have believed that the wooden table had a shine left in it, but there it stood, gleaming as it surely had in its glory days.

"You must be starved," he said, placing the pair of napkin-covered plates that he had carried from town on the hearth. "Hope you like steak and potatoes. They're from the hotel."

Lilleth dropped the sudsy rag in the sink and wiped her hands on her skirt. She closed her eyes and took a slow, savoring breath.

From under the cloth wrappers, the aroma of herbs and spices floated on the air.

"Clark Clarkly, I do believe that you are an angel fallen straight from heaven."

Lilleth crossed the room in a hurry. Instead of collapsing into a fireside chair, she stood before him. Hands on hips, she studied him, cocking her head to the right. Then she wrapped her arms about his ribs in a hug.

For the briefest instant her breasts pressed against his chest. His reaction to that was anything but angelic. Lucky thing she couldn't tell what her embrace had done to him. Things stirred that had no business stirring for a married woman.

He stumbled backward, then hiccuped to cover his reaction.

"I'm sorry," she said, clapping her hands to her cheeks, probably trying to hide a blush. "That was forward."

"I'm hungry. Let's eat." What else could he say? He was starved, had been for sixteen years. No plate of food was going to solve that.

"How are the children doing?" Lilleth sat down and placed a dinner plate on her lap. She uncovered the food, tucked the cloth into the bodice of her dress, then sighed and ate a mouthful of mashed potatoes. "I've neglected them dreadfully today."

He followed her example. "Mary's asleep and Jess is reading. They've both had dinner, the house is warm and the door is locked." There, just now, relief shifted in her eyes. He'd thrown that last out just to see how she would react.

Lils was troubled. Trace's gut told him it was not only her living situation that was the problem. He wondered if her husband had run out not just on his family, but also his debts.

This cabin tucked away in the woods might be an attempt to hide from unscrupulous debt collectors.

Outside, the wind began to blow. It huffed against the windows and rattled the door. It moaned under the eaves and prowled around corners, as if searching for a way inside.

Let it do its best. He'd sealed the place up tight,

even though he'd had to finish by the light of the rising moon.

"Mary misses you, but Jess is doing a fine job of tending her." Trace chewed a bite of steak. "You are not neglecting your children, Lilly. You've worked yourself to the bone for them today."

"So have you." She watched him for a long moment, as if trying to see something deep inside him. She blinked, then seemed to give herself a mental shake. "I can't think of how I will repay you."

He set his plate aside, bent toward her with his elbows on his knees. She crossed her arms over her chest and leaned back in her chair.

"I'd like to get to know you." He already did, of course, and he was a cad for not explaining how. If duty did not stand in his way he'd confess right now. "How did you come to be in Riverwalk?"

He shouldn't have asked, not with weariness shadowing her eyes and dragging at her mouth.

"Oh…well." One of the things he loved about Lilleth was that her face was so open. He'd always been able to read her expression. Just now a flash of relief shaded her eyes. "I wanted a fresh start, for the children. I thought this might be a nice place."

"It is." Finished eating, Trace snapped his napkin from his collar and dropped it on his plate. "I've seen that much in the couple of months that I've been here."

"You're a newcomer, too?"

Giving up that little bit of information about himself couldn't hurt, but he'd better switch the conversation back to her.

He nodded. "Do you have family nearby?"

"My sister." Lilleth turned her face to gaze at the fire. Her cheeks, blushed by the heat of the flames, looked soft...kissable...and not his to kiss. "She's not far away."

Bethany. He remembered her well, of course, even though his attention years ago had been absorbed by her little sister.

"Where did you live before you came to Riverwalk?"

"Here and there. We traveled a lot." She snatched her gaze away from the fire and looked him full in the face. "What about you?"

"Chicago." It was a big town; he could be honest about that, too.

"I spend two weeks in Chicago every year for—" Lilleth's eyes widened for an instant before she looked down, to pick at a spot on her skirt. "My husband had meetings there, so we all went."

It might be angry business partners that she was hiding from.

And she was hiding. Trace was all but certain of it. He wished she would confide in him, even if it would be tough to know her secrets without revealing his own.

Lilleth stood up. She turned her back to the fire,

then sat down on the raised hearth. More curls sprang out of her bun than were contained by it. They clung to her neck in whorls.

He had to look away. It wasn't right to want to put his lips right there, to taste her smooth, fair skin.

"I understand there is a mental hospital here, just outside of town," she said, picking at that spot on her skirt again.

"Hanispree."

He turned his chair so that it faced her.

"Have you been there?" she asked.

He nodded. "I take books to the inmates on occasion."

"Is it a safe facility?" Judging by the look on her face, his answer appeared to be important to her. "To raise the children nearby, I mean. They don't ever escape, do they?"

"Not to my knowledge." He needed to be off this subject. "I don't think the inmates are dangerous so much as unfortunate."

"Well, then…" She let go of her skirt and folded her hands in her lap. She smiled. "That is a relief."

"Let me see your hands."

"Whatever for?"

He didn't answer, just reached over and took them in his. He turned them palm-up.

"You aren't used to this kind of work."

She curled her fingers inward, hiding blisters.

"What needs to be done, needs to be done." She shrugged her shoulders.

"This ought to help."

He reached in his back pocket and withdrew the balm he'd brought from home. Some patients at Hanispree got sores, so he kept it on hand.

She opened her mouth to say something, but in the end did not. She uncurled her hands.

He unscrewed the jar lid. A flowery scent wafted out. He scooped up a dollop of salve with his thumb and rubbed it over her left palm.

Work had taken its toll on her delicate skin. Flipping her hand over, he stroked the lotion from wrist to fingertips.

Her sigh, sounding weary to the bone, made him look up. Her eyes had drifted closed, but half a smile lingered on her lips.

Kissing her would be easy. All he had to do was lean forward two feet and ignore his conscience.

Maybe he should ignore it. A runaway husband didn't deserve the respect of a marriage vow, in Trace's opinion.

He bent closer, just a foot, and stared at her mouth.

That's as close as he got. Until he knew how she viewed her broken wedding vows he couldn't lean forward that further twelve inches and claim what he wanted.

Damn! He couldn't kiss her regardless, not with his own secrets standing in the way.

A sudden gust of wind shook the cabin. Lilleth opened her eyes.

"Clark?" Naturally, she looked astonished to see him so close.

"You've got a smudge of dirt, just there." He wiped her cheek downward to the corner of her lip with his thumb. Its path left a glistening, rose-scented trail on her skin. "That's better, all clean."

She arched a brow, and then closed her eyes once more.

By the time he finished treating her right hand, her breathing had slowed. She'd fallen asleep sitting up in the chair.

"Time to go home, Lils." He whispered. "Stars shine bright...."

He choked back the rest. What if she wasn't deeply asleep? She might recall their nightly farewell even if she didn't remember him.

Lilleth felt as if she was being rocked in a hammock. The hammock smelled like Clark.

The hammock *was* Clark. He carried her, wrapped in his coat, through the woods toward his house. Cold air bit her face where the wind touched it, but she was warm under the wool. Hot, even, where one side of her was tucked tight against his body.

Branches scraped and cracked in the trees overhead. Ice crunched under Clark's boots. His breath turned to fog close to her nose, where she rested her head on his shoulder.

She had been correct about muscle upon muscle. She was not a featherweight, yet he did not appear to be winded.

She ought to walk; her legs were perfectly capable. Somehow, though, she didn't want to.

No one had ever made her feel cherished and protected. Right this moment, Clark did.

He made her feel safe. At last, here was a man who stepped in to help when he didn't have to.

His manner wasn't bold or brave. He didn't have a dozen traits that gallant men had. What he did have was a deep sense of honor.

A woman could trust him.

He'd proved that only moments ago when she had closed her eyes, oblivious to anything but the blissful treatment he was giving her hands. He could have kissed her. In fact, he had wanted to.

She knew enough of men to know when one wanted a kiss…or more.

The strange and startling fact was that she had been disappointed by Clark's gentlemanly behavior. She admired him for it, to be sure, but in truth, she'd wanted his kiss.

She ought to have claimed to be a widow. Now she was stuck as a married woman. If she encouraged a kiss, she would appear a regular trollop. Which she most certainly was not.

A sudden gust spun up from the ground, ripping the coat from her shoulder. Clark turned and walked backward against the wind, tucking the fabric up around her ears as he went.

"Breathing's easier when you back into the wind," he told her.

She touched his face. His cheek was cold, her fingers warm from being sheltered in the coat. The scent of roses lingered on her hand.

He stopped suddenly. Sincere blue eyes blinked at her, both brows arched. His icy breath clouded, mingled with hers, then wisped away.

"Would you think I was wicked if I wished that I was no longer married, so that you could kiss me?"

He looked startled.

"That was bold. I shouldn't have asked." What was wrong with her? What she wanted was not what could be. Even if it could, she had not come to Riverwalk to dally with a man. She was not, and never had been, the dallying type. "Please forgive me."

His arms, firm with rippled muscle, tensed and drew her closer.

"Do you think *I'm* wicked?" he asked.

"No, far from it."

He touched his nose to hers. She tasted his breath on her lips, felt his warmth.

"I've wanted to kiss you since the day I bowled you over on the train platform. And that is the truth. If you think you are wicked, I'm more so."

Something inside her melted. Her bones, certainly, and her flesh.

Even though his lips drew away without ever touching hers, she was quite certain that she had never been so thoroughly kissed in her life.

Chapter Five

Alden Hanispree felt eyes staring at his back. He whipped around, searching the hallway behind him. As always, there was nobody there. At least nobody who could be seen. He hated being alone. Even in his own home, dead people's stares followed him everywhere.

"Go away!" he yelled.

He'd heard that if you asked, they might leave you in peace. Since asking had done no good in the past, he was reduced to screeching.

The lifeless souls following him probably belonged to his parents, and most certainly his brother. He'd never been able to please his parents in life and saw no reason why it should be any different now.

His older brother, Hamilton, born only moments before him, had always been the favorite. He was the son who did everything right. Even on the rare occasion that Alden felt a need to please, his own efforts turned sour.

Poor Alden had taken up with the wrong kind of friends, his parents used to say, trying to excuse his behavior. But Hamilton, with the right kind of friends, got commendations.

His brother's friends were a stuffy lot, though. Alden enjoyed his own companions, wrong kind though they may have been.

Damn them all, where were they now? They knew he hated being alone.

Alden slapped something from his shoulder. An unearthly touch, he supposed.

He pressed his back against the wall, where the tender spot between his shoulder blades didn't feel so vulnerable…so watched.

With a clear view of the hallway he saw that no ghostly presence lurked in the shadows. His tension eased.

Someone would be along shortly and the fear would go away. He wasn't a coward, even though he'd heard it whispered in phantom tones from behind curtains, or coming from closets.

Not a coward, but a sociable person, most comfortable in the presence of others, as many others as he could be with.

Just as soon as he had his hands on what should have been his inheritance, he would have the funds to attract a devoted social circle. Friends who would fawn over him day and night.

All he needed was control of his niece and nephew, and the fortune was his. Their mother would give him any amount of money to see to their well-being.

Footsteps tromped on the long stairway that curved from the grand foyer past the second-floor garden room, then up to the third story, where the bedrooms were.

"Where the hell have you been, Perryman?" Alden snarled, even though he was relieved not to be alone any longer.

"Where do you think, Hanispree?"

Perryman looked like a hawk, with a long, beaked nose and small eyes that were dark, nearly completely black. He was tall, thin, and walked hunched over because he was constantly scanning the ground for bugs. Perryman liked to eat bugs. Any kind would do.

He was the most "wrong kind" of his friends, and the one Alden liked the best.

"Whoring?" He peered up into Perryman's gaunt face.

Alden resented being short and having to always look up to other men. He had spent his life doing it. Naturally, Hamilton had been tall.

"As if I have the time." Perryman glanced about, scanning the floor, which was insulting, since Alden took pains to make sure the servants kept Hanispree Mansion immaculate. "That reward you promised better be a big one. Abstinence is wearing on me."

"It's not even been two days since we visited Willow's." He and Perryman did share a taste for the fallen woman. No messy affections involved with the sordid sort. When passion bordered on barbarity, a whore was happy with an extra coin. "What did you find out?"

"The brats are missing. No one knows anything."

"Especially you!" Alden shouted at his stupid friend, before forcing his voice to a more congenial tone. "I know the brats are missing. There will be no fortune for either of us unless you find out where they went."

"Like I said, nobody knows anything. Maybe we should call on a mystic?" Perryman fluttered his bony fingers in front of Alden's face. "Oo-o-o!"

"Maybe we should use logic." He stepped away from the wall, out from under the taunting fingers. "Use your brain. My nephew and niece are gone. Who would have taken them? Not their mother."

"Nice work hiding her away in Bedlam." Perryman chuckled. "Everyone swallowed that crap you spread about her going to France to grieve."

Nice work indeed, that. Hamilton had planned to spend a big chunk of what ought to have been Alden's inheritance on that Paris trip, before he took ill.

It was pure providence that Mother and Father had given Alden the lunatic house to run. Mistakenly, they had hoped that the responsibility might make him a man like Hamilton.

"So, who else, then?" he asked, thinking out loud.

"Don't know." Perryman irritated him by once again glancing at the floor.

"Her sister, you idiot." His friend was an imbecile.

"Ah, the pretty one who sings?" Perryman's gaze shot up. He licked his lips. "I like that one."

"And where might she have gone?"

"Don't know, Alden. Ask the mystic."

All at once, Alden's hand shot out and upward. He slapped Perryman in the face. He hadn't intended to react that way, but Perryman had disrespected him.

"Sorry, Perryman." But he wasn't sorry. The fool would believe he was, though; he always did. "Think about where she would take them."

Perryman shrugged and rubbed his cheek. "Maybe she didn't believe that Bethany went to France."

"That's smart. I bet you think she took the brats to their mother."

"I was just about to say so."

"Then you need to look for them in Riverwalk. You can be on the next train out of here."

"Or you can. I'm for Willow's."

"I've hired you for the job." He would never admit that he couldn't go near the mental hospital. He'd heard the stories of the ghosts that hover in the halls. "And think about this. Once we get those kids back, you and I will be able to buy Willow's. What do you think about that?"

"I think I'm on the next train to Riverwalk."

* * *

Lilleth blessed the person who had built the cabin with a raised hearth. He must have had babies that needed protecting.

Just now, Mary stood on wobbly legs, watching the flames eat up kindling and logs. Had the hearth been floor level, Lilleth would not get a single thing done, with having to move her away from danger all the time.

As it was, Lilleth found it to be a continual task keeping the child out of harm's way. Small items found on the floor were a fascination to her. The pocket in Lilleth's apron was quickly filling up with items she hadn't noticed before Mary began to creep about on the floor. So far the collection included a cork, a button, a wheel from a broken toy and a triangle of broken glass.

Her respect for Bethany grew by the hour. Raising a toddler took more skill and patience than she could have imagined.

This afternoon, though, her patience was being strained. There was so much she needed to get done to make the cabin livable. But only a moment into a task, Mary would fuss or need to be pulled away from some danger that she found to be fascinating.

Naturally, this made the baby unhappy, so another moment passed while Lilleth tried to make her smile and forget her frustration at not being allowed to injure herself.

This was not easy, since Mary was teething. Her rare bouts of contentment lasted for only a moment… unless she was being held.

How did mothers get a blessed thing done?

Jess helped, but he was a child himself and shouldn't be burdened with the care of his sister. He did spend a great deal of time playing in the woods, but fear of Alden kept him within sight of the cabin.

When he tired of exploring, he helped out at the lending library under the watchful eye of—she sighed and felt silly for it—of Mr. Clark Clarkly.

"No, no, Mary." Lilleth uncurled the chubby fingers from the fireplace poker, then cleaned the ash off an instant before the baby plunged them into her mouth. "That's not for you, sweetie."

Evidently, fireplace pokers were one more thing that had to be stored where Mary couldn't get to them. The cabin would soon be dotted from one wall to the other with hooks holding dangerous objects out of Mary's reach.

"Please, Lord, keep this child safe until I learn mothering," Lilleth whispered, looking up.

Mary's eyes watered, her lip quivered. She plopped down on the floor, crying.

"Poor dolly, come here, then." Lilleth set aside the washrag she had been using to scrub the table, and picked Mary up. "How about if Auntie sings to you?"

She shouldn't sing, but really, it was all she knew to do to comfort the unhappy child. She hadn't the motherly skills that Bethany had, but she had been known to quiet fretful beasts and belligerent theater-goers with her voice.

She sat in the chair beside the fire, the very one Clark had sat in a few days before, when he had rubbed lotion on her hands. She imagined that the scent of him still lingered on it.

What was happening to her? She had never longed for the scent of a man. No indeed, she'd kept males as far away from her person as she could without appearing uncivil.

For some reason, she wanted to be civil to Clark... very civil.

There was something about him that set him apart from other men. His kindness, to be sure, but there was more than that.

She liked the way he smelled. She was sure to like the way he tasted, were she given the chance.... Also, there was the way he looked at her when he wasn't aware that she noticed.

"Auntie's becoming muddleheaded." She settled Mary in her arms. The baby stuck her thumb in her mouth. Lilleth stroked the moisture from her niece's round, pink cheek. "What can Auntie sing to soothe you?"

Baby songs weren't in her repertoire, but she remembered a few that her mother used to sing before unfaithful men had snatched away her joy.

"I see the moon and the moon sees me," she sang.

It felt good to let her voice out. The odds were remote that anyone would hear her, even more remote that they would recognize her by it. "The moon sees somebody I'd like to see. God bless the moon and God bless me, and God bless the somebody I'd like to see."

She barely finished the short verse before Mary fell asleep. "And God bless your momma, little one," she whispered into Mary's delicate ear. "I'm going to see her very soon."

Not much could feel better than holding this precious bundle, soothing her, watching her sleep. Still, there was work to be done, and sitting here listening to the fire crackle while she watched Mary's peaceful breathing wasn't getting it done.

Outside, the sun shone. Water dripped from icicles; chunks of snow slid off the roof and hit the ground with a soft splat.

In town folks would be taking advantage of the respite in the weather to scurry about their business. Here in her little cabin the woods, though, Lilleth would take a moment to feel the warm, sleepy weight in her arms and steal a second to daydream.

It was true what she had confessed to Mary—she was becoming muddled. She never daydreamed, at least not much, and not about men.

Clark's near kiss had certainly changed that. Not only did she daydream about his mouth, his scent and the feel of his beard stubble against her fingertips, at night she dreamed about things she should never be pondering with a baby on her lap.

With a sigh, Lilleth looked for a place to set Mary down. The sooner she had the cabin cleaned up, the sooner she would be out of Clark's home and the sooner she would get her emotional balance back.

Life was about the practical. For instance, where would she lay Mary down? The hearth would be warm but dangerous. The table was clean but a bit slanted, and Mary might roll off. The bed was unthinkable.

A quiet knock sounded on the front door. The latch lifted and the door opened wide.

Silhouetted by sunshine stood the object of her muddleheadedness, carrying the answer to her prayer in his arms.

Clark closed the door with his foot, then set a wood cradle beside her chair.

Trace stared at the blank sheet of paper on his desk. He tapped his idle pen on the blotter.

In his mind's eye he saw Lilleth in the moonlight, wrapped in his jacket. He felt again the way her weight fitted into his arms, the curve of her hip and the shape of her thigh.

Had she not been married, he would have kissed her…and thoroughly. He'd enjoyed some kisses in his life, but not a single one compared to the one he'd nearly had with Lilleth. In his mind's eye he saw her lips again in the instant that she touched her fingers to his face.

He had fully believed that moonlight brushed her lips and that starlight frolicked in her eyes. That time had turned back on itself.

The very last thing he had expected was to be resisting her kiss.

Now nothing would be the same until he had one in the flesh.

He'd never been a man to enjoy a parade of meaningless lovers, but he'd hadn't lived a monk's life, either. He had known a few women. Two had been foisted upon him by his ever so helpful brothers, another by his sister. One had been his own choice.

Four women, and all of them lovely. It was just that somehow he could never commit his heart to them.

He suspected that the reason for that was at this very moment soaking in his bathtub in a room just off the kitchen. Her pretty wet body could only be forty feet and a closed door away.

No wonder the blank sheet of paper stared up at him. His pen could do nothing but smear a black blob on the blotter.

Trace shook himself. He'd sat down at the desk with a purpose, and that purpose had not been to imagine what Lilleth looked like lying naked in his bathtub.

It had been to make note of his latest findings on

Hanispree Mental Hospital, and wire them to the family. Three days had passed since his last correspondence, and they were bound to wonder. It was a long-standing company rule to wire daily.

He needed to be able to tell them something other than that there was a woman in his bathtub, though.

Lilleth aside, he'd broken another cardinal family rule: never become personally involved in a case. His job was to observe and report. Anything more than that created problems.

He had come to Riverwalk to uncover secrets and write an exposé that would shut Hanispree down. The inmates could then be sent to institutions where they would be cared for.

The trouble was, how many of those inmates would even survive the care given at the asylum long enough to be transferred? When old ladies shivered in their beds, when previously vital human beings looked to be bones more than flesh, and when otherwise intelligent brains began to rot, someone had to step in.

Clark Clarkly was that someone.

If a cardinal rule was bent, the family would survive. The victims of Hanispree might not.

Darkness pressed upon the library windows, and the temperature was falling. Tonight, he would be bringing food and lighting fires.

Fortunately, he would no longer have to waste time sneaking keys from the nurse's desk. He'd configured one of his own that would open every door in the place.

The Ballentines were gifted with skills that most families were not. Making a universal key was something he had learned to do at the age of fifteen. He could do it in his sleep, if he were getting any.

Trace stared down at his paper…still blank. The stain on the blotter had grown to the size of a silver dollar.

From the back of the house, Clark heard the bathroom door open. Feminine footsteps padded up the rear stairs.

What would his houseguest be wearing? Trace set down his pen to prevent accidentally bending the tip.

A practical flannel gown that covered her from neck to toe? Something filmier that stroked the curve of her breast and caressed the line of her thigh?

Or just a short towel that left her legs and arms bare? If so, drops of scented water might linger on her skin, catching the light of the lantern that dimly illuminated the stairs.

If that was the case he'd be astounded, since she had just tiptoed into a room she shared with two sleeping children. When it came to Lils, apparently his imagination had no sense or reason.

Flannel then. But he had never once, in the last sixteen years, ever imagined that she would be here with only that one layer of fabric between her flesh and his dreams.

Trace stood up. He shook himself, which seemed to be becoming a habit. Lilleth would go her way soon and he would go his. That's how it had to be.

He went to the kitchen, put on the heavy coat that hung beside the back door, and picked up the bag of food he had prepared earlier.

He stepped out into the cold.

Lilleth heard the back door close. She tiptoed past the bed where the children slept, and looked out the window into the small yard below.

Just as he had on previous nights, Clark made some kind of excursion into the dark and the cold. The full moon cast his shadow on the snow. Once again, he carried a big bag. Tonight he took his ax.

Lilleth hugged her robe tight about her and tapped her foot.

It didn't take a lot of figuring to know where he had gone. Off to chop firewood for some woman, unless she missed her guess.

"Lilleth Preston, you are a mountain of a fool," she mumbled, frowning as Clark's long and…no mistake about it…confident strides took him around a corner.

Who was Clark Clarkly, really?

He was a puzzle, and it was no business of hers to try and figure him out. She had no claim on him. Whether there was or was not a woman in his life, it was no concern of hers.

A ninny was what she was. Without knowing his attachments, she had mooned over him. Had come close to kissing him! She had let herself ride a magic carpet of wishes, imagining that he was her hero. That she might be special to him.

But then again, from what she knew of Clark, everyone was special to him. Maybe the woman he was carrying his ax for was just someone in need of charity.

In the end, Lilleth could not guess where he was going tonight. What she did know was that her hair was wet and she was going downstairs to sit by the fire and let it dry.

She kissed Jess on the cheek. He stirred and smiled in his sleep. Maybe he thought it was his mother's kiss. Lilleth did the same to Mary, inhaling the sweet baby breath that grazed her nose.

Downstairs, she picked a book from the library shelf, then settled in the chair that Clark slept in at night.

This chair did smell like him. There was no denying that he was her hero, spending night after night on spindly legged furniture while she and the children snuggled in his bed.

She spread her hair over her shoulders so that the heat of the flames could reach it.

She opened the book. Maybe she ought to have been more selective rather than taking the first volume she touched.

"'Miss Fairhaven and the Dashing Blade,'" she read out loud. "The title is featherheaded." Certainly she would be bored to sleep by page two. She ought to get up and select another, but she was settled and her hair arranged just so.

In time, she did get sleepy. Just when the Dashing Blade had cornered Miss Fairhaven in a convent closet, after having rescued her from brigands, losing her in a creepy forest, then discovering her again in a deserted town and chasing her into the nunnery, Lilleth's eyes grew too heavy to continue.

Drat! What was Miss Fairhaven going to do?

Meet the Dashing Blade at the county fair, naturally. There he was; she saw him behind her closed eyelids. He found her crouched behind the kissing booth. She had been hiding from someone, but probably not the Dashing Blade.

He offered her a slice of peach pie and she came along quite willingly.

"Hey, Lils," he said. "Let's go sit on the bridge and watch the fireworks."

Miss Fairhaven must have thought that was a fine idea. She skipped along beside him, looking much younger and happier than she had hiding in the closet of the nunnery.

They sat down on the bridge, hip to hip, eating pie and listening to the creek gurgle under their feet. Miss Fairhaven couldn't remember ever feeling so content, sitting here with Trace and watching fireworks burst over the fields like a million fairies dancing in wild abandon.

Trace held her hand.

"Be my king," she whispered to him. "And I'll be your fairy queen. We'll swirl away into the night and live blissfully ever after."

Trace bent his lips to her ear to whisper something.

"Lilly?" A big warm hand touched her shoulder.

Hazy, half in and out of sleep, Lilleth opened her eyes.

"Trace?" She blinked, stared, then sighed. "Oh, Clark, it's you."

"Disappointed?" He straightened his glasses on his nose, then pulled up a chair and sat across from her, knee to knee.

"Not at all…just surprised. I was dreaming."

"Your robe." He cleared his throat and tipped his head in the direction of the garment. "It's slipped."

"Oh!" She bolted up in the chair. Miss Fairhaven and her oh so Dashing Blade fell out of her lap and onto the floor. Lilleth tugged gray flannel over her shoulder and hugged it tight to her neck. The lace gown she wore under it covered her as thoroughly as a shadow. Clark had just been privy to a sight not seen by any other man.

Heat blazed in her cheeks. Her face must look aflame. She was disconcerted, flustered, by what she had exposed to him.

But it was her immodest mind that turned her crimson with mortification. She studied his face, watching for a reaction.

Did he like what he had seen?

"Who is Trace?" he asked, shoving his glasses to the bridge of his nose, as though her charms had gone unnoticed.

"Clark." She let go of the robe choking her throat. It sagged open, but more modestly this time. "You've just seen more of me than…never mind."

She'd nearly forgotten she was married, and not a woman who had experienced only one, exceptionally brief, encounter with a man. She would have to be more careful in the future.

"You thought I was him, just for that second." At least he had the decency to be fighting a grin. "Just wondering, is all."

"I didn't think you were him. You woke me from a dream."

"You were dreaming…of him?"

"I was not. The Dashing Blade was flitting in and out of my dream, if you have to know." How odd that for a brief second he appeared disappointed. "Trace was a boy I knew a long time ago. We were childhood friends, that's all."

"Childhood friends make the longest-lasting impressions. Mine did. What about this Trace fellow? He must have been darn special, since you dreamed about him after all this time."

"He was." What could she say? He had been her everything and it had devastated her when she had been dragged away in the night, crying her heart out. The tears had gone on for weeks. She'd become physically ill. As a result, she hadn't allowed herself to have a friend that she cared for so deeply again. "He was my first and dearest friend. He was also my last."

"I'm sorry, Lilly." Clark reached for her hands and held them in his. He rubbed her palms with his thumbs.

The robe gaped open another inch, but he probably didn't notice.

Chapter Six

Trace walked toward the mercantile with sunshine warming his shoulders and slush soaking his boots.

It had been three and a half days since he had wakened Lilleth from her dream. Seventy-four hours of joy and torment.

Lace under flannel!

Trace felt off balance with that revelation. It was becoming a challenge to his self-control to remain Clark Clarkly.

Luckily, Lilleth and the children would be moving into the cabin tomorrow. Maybe then he'd be able to concentrate on his exposé instead of constantly watching Lilleth out of the corner of his eye. Maybe then he'd remember that a blank sheet of paper required words to be written on it.

Deep in his thoughts, Trace nearly ran down a stick-thin man walking past the front door of the Riverwalk Hotel.

This time it had not been intentional. The man was not watching where he went. He gazed down, scanning the boardwalk, side to side. Maybe he'd lost something.

"I beg your pardon," Trace murmured, passing by the stranger and glancing down to make sure he didn't trample the thing that the man was searching for.

A beetle, lured from his autumn hiding place by the warm day, scurried over a cracked wood plank, so Trace stepped wide of it. The thin man cocked his head in apparent interest in the bug.

Strange man.

A moment later Trace spotted Lilleth with the children a few shops down, at the milliner's. She carried Mary on her hip and pointed to some lacy object in the window. The baby reached for the glass and Lilleth smiled. She said something he was too far away to hear.

Jess knelt beside his mother's skirt, trying to coax a stray cat to come and smell his hand. Lilleth went into the store, but Jess remained outside, while the cat inched toward his fingers.

What wouldn't Trace give to have them as his family! He'd give everything, everything but his calling. And that was only because innocent lives depended on him.

Well, then, since he couldn't give her Trace Ballentine, he would give her what he could. Just now, as Clark, he bumbled his way to the mercantile to buy her a bed, one for Jess, too.

Having provided the Gordons with plenty of firewood and a place to sleep, he would be free to continue his quest to shut down Hanispree. He could not allow anything to be more important to him than seeing each and every one of the inmates transferred to a respectable institution.

With his hand on the doorknob of the mercantile, Trace turned moon-eyed, to see if Lilleth had come back outside. At some point he'd have to learn not to do that. Watching her smile, studying the arch of her brow and discreetly watching her bosom rise and fall with her breathing could only end in misery.

His Lils was no longer his Lils.

He began to step over the threshold of the store, but stopped dead still. Warm air from inside washed over his face while the cold knob chilled his fist.

The narrow-faced stranger was staring at Jess. The man had gone into the alley between the milliner and bakery. He peeked his head around the corner of the building, blatantly spying on the boy.

Strange man…strange behavior.

Trace closed the door on the warmth. He hurried down the steps to get between the stranger and Jess.

All at once an arm snaked around Trace's shoulder and a man's weight sagged against him. Alcohol reeked from his jacket but not on his breath.

"Brother, can you spare a fellow a dime?"

* * *

Cooper Ballentine leaned against Trace, draping his full weight across Trace's shoulders. Cooper was the most dramatic of his brothers, and the only one to have been born with blond hair and brown eyes. Had he not taken up the family calling, Trace was sure that Cooper would have made a life for himself onstage.

"Abner's hitting the swill a little early, don't you think?" Trace spoke to his brother, but kept his eye on the man watching Jess.

"Never too early for good ole Ab." Cooper slurred his speech to perfection. "'Sides, I like Ab."

Cooper tripped and Trace hauled him back up. As boys, they had perfected various falls and landings. If one looked closely, Clark Clarkly and Abner Welchtin reacted to gravity in an identical manner.

"Tell me what you're doing here later, Coop." From across the street Clark watched Jess tip his head to one side, unaware of the watcher, being absorbed as he was in the slow progress of the cat. "There's a man watching the boy over there, the one with the cat. I need you to follow him, see where he goes."

"Need a drink in the worst way, mister," Cooper said in a loud voice, and all but drooled on Trace's shirt. "Jus' a dime."

"Find your own dime, you swillbelly."

Cooper detached himself from Trace, then stumbled in the direction of the stranger.

"I ain't no swill…swill—whatever that was." Cooper dropped to the dirt, got up and dusted off his knees, then stumbled toward the alley. "Might be for a dime, though."

Not likely. His brother couldn't drink, ever since he'd gotten sick from it as a kid. Cooper cursed that day as much as their mother blessed it.

"Hey, mister!" Cooper weaved his way toward the watcher. "Can you spare a dime…just one?"

The man disappeared down the alley, trying to evade Abner Welchtin, who stumbled behind him, determined in his pursuit of a coin.

As much as Trace didn't care to hear the reprimand that Cooper had most likely come to deliver from the family, he was glad his brother had arrived. Cooper could sniff out a man as reliably as Jess's stray cat was likely to sniff out fish.

Jess stood up. The cat dashed off. The boy stretched his arms over his head, looking young, carefree and ignorant of potential danger. With a slow pivot he went into the milliner's.

One thing was certain. The Gordons would not be walking home alone.

Chances were, the stranger was just a man interested in watching a boy catch a cat. But what if there was more to it?

Trace had had a niggling feeling that Lilleth was

frightened of something. Now, with someone watching, the odds were not good enough for Trace to keep his distance.

"I got a creepy feeling, Ma," Jess whispered while Lilleth switched Mary from one hip to the other. "Couldn't look up to see anything, but the itchy twitchy was there, right in the middle of my back. And the cat was skittish."

"Cats are naturally skittish, especially around strangers."

And Alden may have deduced that it was she who had taken his wards. Where would he look but Riverwalk, even if he did fear being stalked by the restless dead?

She intended to free Bethany if it took her last breath. Alden would know that. With his fortune at stake, he might be bolder than Lilleth had expected.

"He didn't seem like a stranger to me. Ouch!" Jess untangled his hair from his sister's chubby fist. "It was like the cat's known me all along. Do you think I might keep him?"

That would be unwise. Life was in such an upheaval now, how could they offer shelter to a cat?

They couldn't possibly. No, the appropriate answer would be no.

"If you catch him, Jess, you can keep him."

His eyes lit up in a way she hadn't seen in some time. True happiness radiated from them. For all the world, they looked like Bethany's used to, before her life fell apart.

"No" would have been the appropriate answer, but "yes" was the right answer. Jess still needed to catch the creature, after all. In her heart Lilleth hoped he did. It might distract him from his troubles for a little while.

"Thanks, Ma!" Looking like the happy boy he ought to be, Jess dashed from the store.

"Don't forget to be—" she called after him. She caught herself from saying "careful."

A child shouldn't carry the burden of watching over his shoulder for danger. She would do that for him, although if it came to it, all Alden had to do was complain to the law that she had kidnapped his wards. They would be taken from her, all neat and legal.

She would have the devil of a time getting them away again.

"Good luck, Jess," she said to the slamming door. "I hope you catch the kitty."

Lilleth purchased earmuffs for Mary and followed Jess outside. The cat had vanished.

"You'll find him. Maybe tomorrow." She glanced about, pretending to search for the feline, scanning shadows and doorways for someone who might have been watching Jess.

To her relief, the only one watching was Clark.

As luck would have it, they seemed to be headed in the same direction at the same time.

"Good afternoon, Mr. Clarkly." Gracious, but when was the last time her smile had ever felt so warm? "It's lovely in town this afternoon."

His smile in return was sweet, sincere, and if she was not mistaken, just a little bit wicked.

"May I walk you home, Mrs. Gordon?"

There it was; just the slightest blush gave away his thoughts. He wanted more than the kiss they had nearly shared.

"I'd be delighted." And didn't she want more than that, as well?

"It looks like there'll be snow before morning." He glanced at the sky, then down an alley. "We'll have to build a big roaring fire for our last night together."

"Indeed, Mr. Clarkly. I can't think of anything I'd like more."

She blushed. He blushed. They looked away from each other, while Jess watched for his cat to come out of hiding.

As it turned out, it did snow and they did build a fire. A huge raging one…that they shared with Cooper.

No fewer than ten times in the past hour—Trace counted every one of them—Cooper turned his head and arched an inquisitive brow at him.

Luckily, Lilleth hadn't noticed. She seemed absorbed by her thoughts while she stared at the fire. Once again she seemed troubled, and he doubted that it was because of Cooper's charming presence.

Trace had outright lied to her about who his brother was. He'd introduced Cooper as the cousin of a friend from far away. While it was unlikely that she would remember him, one never knew what might spark a memory.

Cooper flirted with Lilleth the same way he did all women. His behavior was more annoying than ever, since the object of his attention was Lils.

Lilleth countered his advances as expertly as a tennis player returning a volley. Her interest in Cooper's game lasted only a few minutes before she went back to quietly staring at the flames.

A skilled flirt! There might be more to his Lils than the sweet child she had been and the abandoned woman she had become. The less Trace knew the better, really, but there was a puzzle here. Puzzles tended to eat at him until he solved them.

"Gentlemen, if you'll excuse me," she said all at once, standing up and smoothing a fold in her skirt. "All of a sudden I'm done in."

Not with weariness, Trace guessed, but done in with something. Could be Cooper, but he doubted it. Ladies usually enjoyed his attention.

"Do I need to ask why you're here?" Trace asked, after he heard the bedroom door close. "Hope you've found a place to stay. I've got the chair."

"Damn Grange meeting," Cooper grumbled. "Guess I've got the kitchen table."

"Tried it. Don't envy you, little brother."

"Younger by eleven months hardly counts."

"Younger is always younger." Trace shrugged, grinned, and stretched his boots toward the fire.

"The folks sent me to check on you. You know how they get when no work is sent in. It's been a more than a week since we heard anything from you. Mother is sure you're lying helpless in a ditch. Pop thinks you've taken up the fast life."

"This case is complicated. It's going to take some time."

Cooper leaned forward, his elbows on his knees. "So, why am I the cousin of some distant acquaintance?"

"Didn't you recognize her?"

"No." Cooper shrugged. "Real pretty, though."

"That's Lilleth Preston."

Cooper sat up straight in his chair. "Your long-lost little girlfriend? The one you were so sweet on it nearly killed you?"

Trace nodded.

"What the blazes is she doing in your house?"

"Hiding, I think." Trace kicked off his boots and let the flames warm his socks. He glanced out the front window. Snow drifted past in lazy, swirling flakes. Too much of it might prevent Lilleth from moving tomorrow. "Don't worry, Coop, she doesn't know who I am."

"Wouldn't expect her to. It's been a long time." Cooper flexed his fingers between his knees. "Besides, you're uglier now than you were as a kid."

Trace ignored the comment, because he didn't feel like spending fifteen minutes exchanging barbs.

"I knew who she was the second after I knocked her over."

"Not everyone remembers every detail of their lives.... Really? You knocked her down?"

"Had to. I was Clark."

Cooper kicked off his boots and tossed them beside Trace's. "You better be careful. The folks are counting on you to get things done here. Hanispree is important."

"I haven't forgotten. Rescuing the innocent and saving the family from financial ruin...I get all that."

"Maybe not quite ruin, but times have been hard. This exposé means a lot to us. That's why they gave the job to Clark Clarkly."

"I'm not in trouble. You can relay that to the folks."

"Why'd you have me trail that ghoul?" Cooper yawned and stretched. "Is he involved with Lilleth Preston?"

"Can't be sure. I saw him staring at her son and it gave me a bad feeling."

"Creepy fellow ate a bug." Cooper shivered. "He

finally tossed me a dime before he went into Mrs. O'Hara's. I left it in the dirt. Pity the poor working girl who has to service him."

"Thanks, Cooper. I don't know if he is a threat to Lilleth, but at least I know where he is."

"I'll tell the folks you didn't die in a ditch or become a libertine. Just send them something so I don't have to come back and sleep on your table again." Cooper stood up, stretched and rubbed his eyes. "I'm getting some shut-eye. Make sure you don't snore."

Trace stood up in turn. "I'll get you a blanket."

He mounted the stairs, his steps muffled by his socks, while Cooper went into the kitchen and closed the door.

A lucky thing for Trace, as his brother was the one who snored like a freight train.

He glanced up the staircase and saw a shadow drift across the hall. Not a creepy bug-eating creepy one, though.

This one had hair that tumbled halfway down her back. Masses of red curls glowed in the dim light of the hall lantern. Bare pink toes peeked out from under the flannel robe that she hugged tightly across her chest.

She didn't see him standing on the steps because she was gazing out the window, watching the snow fall. He stood still for a full minute, taking in the sight of her. His very own miracle, or curse, depending on how one looked at it, standing in his hallway, wearing a lacy shift under her worn flannel robe.

Her breath fogged the glass and she wiped it away with her fist.

"Can't sleep?" he asked, letting her know he was there. "Is something wrong?"

She turned to look at him and shook her head. Lantern light caught the pretty line of her jaw, the arch of her brow and the slight upward curve of her lips.

"What could be, really?" She flipped a tumble of curls away from her eye, and her robe fell open. "The snow's coming down and the children and I are safe and warm inside, thanks to you."

Lilleth grasped her hair and began to braid it. Trace suddenly adored braids. Their creation involved both of a woman's hands and left her robe to part completely.

"I love a snowy night," she said, her fingers moving slowly through her hair. "The quiet, the stillness… It's pristine. Everything is snug inside, so very peaccful."

Not only did Trace adore braids, he now thought highly of snow. But lantern light moved to the top of the things he admired most.

When Lilleth turned sideways to gaze out the window again, flickering shadows licked at her lace gown and dappled delicate flower etchings on her skin.

For Trace, the world narrowed to a single point.
He could hardly catch a breath, watching Lilleth in
profile—more exactly, watching one breast in profile. Illuminated softly, it moved with her braiding.
Up and down with the twisting of her hair, followed
by a jiggle when she yanked the tresses tight.

Her nipple pressed against the confining lace. The
lamp's glow lathed the firm little bud, gold over pink.

"It's beautiful, don't you think?" she asked.

"I've never seen anything quite like it." He thought
his voice actually croaked. He ought to do the noble
thing and point out the problem with her clothing.

Didn't want to, but if he stood here much longer,
drooling like a hungry dog, he'd do something he'd
regret…a little bit, at least.

"The snow, that is." He made a Clarklike gesture
with his hands. "Your robe. It's come open again."

"It seems to have a mind of its own sometimes."

Lilleth closed it up, but not before he caught a
glimpse of both lush breasts.

Wind howled in the shutters outside, rattling
them. Common sense abandoned him and he rushed
forward.

He lifted Lilleth up, his thumbs and fingers sup-
porting where her underarms met the tender curve of
her torso. Her breasts skimmed his chest. The scents
of flowers and flesh filled him. Her cheek rested
against his for half an instant, smooth against the

stubble of his beard. She turned her face, her mouth nearly grazing his lips.

"There's a very good chance that I'm a widow," she gasped.

He kissed her gently, reverently...for a respectable second. Then heat flashed through him, burning him with the ache of the empty years he had longed for her.

He nipped at her lips, then devoured them, because he was starved. Hunger that had not begun to be satisfied made him senseless to the snow, the wind, the sleeping children and his snoring brother.

Life narrowed to this one moment, where Lilleth returned his passion, heat upon heat. Where pure, white-hot lust made anything else irrelevant and convinced him that she was, in all probability, a widow. No man would ever leave this woman willingly.

He backed her against the wall and slid her slowly down the front of him. Through his worn flannel shirt, her heavy breathing pressed her to him, heart to heart. Her plush breasts with tight, swollen buds grazed a path downward.

He nuzzled her neck, inhaling the scent of her skin, of the spirit of Lilleth.

She moaned and whispered Clark's name. That alone should have been enough for him to let go of her. Damn it, she didn't even know who he was.

But he couldn't because his gray life had suddenly

burst into color, confetti that flew about his mind in wild confusion.

He buried his face in the softly twining curls at her ear.

"Lils," he whispered.

She stiffened and shoved his shoulders.

Oh, damn, had he said that out loud? Clearly he had. She blinked at him in confusion.

"What was that you called me?"

"It doesn't matter." He stepped away from her, feeling sick at heart.

He had wanted her so badly that he had been willing to believe a lie. Her husband might well be dead...but he might not.

"Forgive me, Lilly, I hardly know what to say. My actions were not gentlemanly...but it won't happen again."

Not gentlemanly? They were cowardly and weak. They were the actions of a selfish idiot.

"I do beg your pardon." He turned, taking the stairs down two at a time.

She groaned. He was certain of that.

"No need to be all that sorry," he thought she said.

No doubt he had misunderstood.

Chapter Seven

Lilleth had moved out of Clark's house as soon as she had forced down her last bite of breakfast pastry.

Now, four hours later, she drew aside the curtain over the window beside the front door of the cabin. She gazed out at last night's dusting of snow. Two sets of footprints led away from the porch, one large and one small: Clark's and Jess's.

Clark had come by earlier to pick up Jess and help him catch his cat. His offer to accompany her nephew had been beyond welcome, since she could not have allowed the boy to go to town alone, and she didn't want to take Mary out in the cold.

Things were as awkward between her and Clark this afternoon as they had been this morning. At breakfast, she couldn't quite meet his eye and he couldn't quite speak a coherent sentence.

It was almost as though the air between them pulsed red with embarrassment. To suggest that maybe she was a widow made her sound like a desperate strumpet. He must think she was ready to spring upon him at any moment.

There must have been some kind of spell lurking in the hallway. What other explanation could there be for what had happened?

She'd wanted his kiss. Only a born and bred fool would deny it. How was she to guess that it would ignite the way it had? That it would burn up her good sense.

Last night Lilleth had not been very smart. Had things not fallen apart when Clark called her Trace Ballentine's pet name for her, he'd have soon discovered that she hadn't the knowledge of intimacy that a widow would have.

While not a virgin in the true sense of the word, her one, exceptionally brief sexual experience, born out of pure curiosity, had left her with more questions than answers. Barely out of her teens, she had wanted to know what drove her mother to take man after man into her bed. After the twenty seconds Lilleth had allowed a handsome young fellow under her skirt, she was more baffled than ever.

Last night, Clark had cleared up a great deal of the mystery.

Living in his house had been a sanctuary, and she would be forever grateful. But she had moved out not a moment too soon.

There were things about Clark Clarkly that puzzled her. There was something just below the surface of the man that she should be able to grasp but could not.

Here in her own home she would regain her balance.

"Mary, isn't this dandy? A place all our own."

The toddler, sitting on the newly polished floor, banged a spoon on top of a pot. Lilleth sat on the floor beside her. It seemed impossible that it had been little more than a week since the floor had been covered with grime instead of polish.

Lilleth picked up a ladle and banged it on the pot in time with Mary's spoon.

"Here, like this." She captured Mary's round little fist and helped her tap the pot. "I used to open my show with this tune."

The tempo of the spoon and the ladle made Lilleth tap her knee on the floor to the rhythm. It couldn't hurt to sing the song softly, just under her breath.

"Mamma," Mary announced.

"Soon, little lambie. You'll see your mother soon."

Tonight, in fact, after she had the children bedded down for the evening, Lilleth intended to venture out. There had to be a way to get to Bethany.

Walking, bold as brass, into the hospital was out of the question. If Alden did suspect that she was in Riverwalk, he would have the staff watching for her.

More than a dozen times, she had longed to ask Clark if he had come across Bethany when he delivered his lending books to the hospital. It would be a comfort to know that he had seen her, that she was coping.

"I can't ask him that, though, can I, little Mary? Our safety depends upon keeping our secrets." Lilleth touched Mary's short curly locks. The hair was so soft she could barely feel it swirl about her fingers. "It's not that I don't think Clark is trustworthy, but this is something we'll have to do on our own."

"Ba…bo," Mary cooed, and smiled.

"I know I can you trust to keep silent." Lilleth stood up and walked to the fireplace. She picked up the poker and urged new life into the flames.

It would be bone-chilling tonight, but probably not snowing. There would be no help for it but to bundle up and venture out into the darkness.

This particular night would be ideal, since there would be no moon. She would be able to poke about the hospital grounds with slim chance of being seen.

Poking about was her only goal for tonight, though. As much as she longed to burst inside to free her sister, like a dime novel gunfighter with weapons blazing, she would have to wait. First, she needed to study the building and the grounds, and then she would figure a way in and out.

Lilleth sat down on the hearth and warmed her back.

"Don't you worry, baby, you'll be in your mama's arms in a bang and a thrash."

An hour later, the front door burst open, blowing in Jess, Clark and a rush of frigid air.

"The cat got this close, Ma!" Jess tugged off his hat and shimmied out of his coat. He tossed them on the hearth and then spread his arms wide. "Clark says he'll come to me next time, sure. I can't rush him, though. It needs to be the cat's own choice, else he'll only run away first chance he gets. I'm hungry. Clark brought dinner from the hotel."

Clark stood beside the closed cabin door, holding several items wrapped in cloth. Steam and the aroma of fried chicken, along with other enticing scents, wafted out of the linens.

She would have to learn to cook, and soon, or the children might starve. She couldn't expect Clark to feed them every day.

When she took the food from his hands, he looked as nervous as any man she had ever seen.

Or maybe not. Thinking back on last night, which she had done dozens upon dozens of times today, frightened was about the last thing he had looked. Had he not called her Lils, they might have done things in the hallway that were meant for the bed-room.

In the end, that name, that endearment, had startled her out of her haze of passion. Clark's voice had sounded like an echo of Trace Ballentine's, older to be sure, but an echo all the same.

"Will you join us for dinner, Clark?" she asked.

"No, but thanks. I've got sorting to do in the library." He straightened his glasses on his nose and shrugged his shoulders, one then the other.

Lilleth set the food on the table.

"Go ahead and eat, Jess. Feed Mary, too, will you?" She settled the baby in a chair and tied her in place with a strip of cloth.

"Clark, I'd like a word with you on the porch."

"Oh, yes. I suppose the sorting can—yes, Lilly, to be sure." He followed her outside and she closed the door behind them.

A gust of cold wind ruffled the hem of her skirt. It tugged Clark's hair and snapped a wavy strand across his forehead.

"It's about last night," she said, and wrapped her arms about her ribs for warmth. "What you must think of me. I acted the regular trollop."

"You were lovely, Lilly, and I was an unprincipled devil." He shoved the hair back from his face to reveal arched brows pushing rows of lines to his hairline.

"The trollop most sincerely apologizes to the devil."

"The devil most sincerely apologizes to the trollop." He smiled. A dimple winked at her. "But seriously, Lilly, you are no trollop."

"Perhaps there was just something in the air."

"Something that took us both by surprise." He blinked and nodded.

"We'll have to be on guard for surprises from now on."

"Diligently, so they won't surprise us again."

"Well, I do feel better, now that we've set things straight," she said, but wondered about the sad little ache in her heart. "Won't you stay for dinner?"

"The good thing about sorting is that it never complains about having to wait."

He opened the door. Heat rushed out. Lamplight spilled over the porch to point a finger at the setting sun.

She walked inside and he came in behind her, closing the door on the falling night.

Trace picked up his ax, swung it over his shoulder and stepped off the back porch of the lending library.

Damn, it was cold. His clothes all but crackled with it.

He wished that he could have remained in Lilleth's cabin, where heat from the fire, good conversation and a full belly made him linger far later than he should have.

Unlike the night before, where the thing that was in the air had spun him like a top and then smashed him on his head, where passion had beheaded common sense and nearly exposed him, tonight had been a night for comfort and quiet friendship.

And really, friendship had been his and Lils's bond way back when. Their attachment had been between hearts. Until last night, passion had been an innocent dream of the future. As children, they hadn't even begun to understand it.

In those days they had shared romantic vows and promises along with one sweet, chaste and heart-wrenching kiss.

Lilleth Preston was his past. Lilly Gordon was his friend. That's all there could ever be, and he would learn to deal with it.

By damn he would.

Cooper had left this morning before breakfast and agreed to report to the family that Trace had been bedridden with some illness or another. In return, Trace had vowed to write all night and day. So far his ink bottle remained corked and his page blank.

He and Jess had made good progress with the cat, though.

Clark shook himself. He had a calling and a goal. He would do well to remember that he was first and always an investigative journalist.

That's exactly why he walked to the mental hospital by way of Mrs. O'Hara's. The skinny bug-eater presented a mystery…a mystery that Trace had every intention of investigating.

With an icy breeze pushing from behind, it took him only a few minutes to reach Mrs. O'Hara's. Her red lantern swayed and cast shifting shards of light over the porch and out onto the road.

This late at night most of Riverwalk's citizens

were asleep. The brothel appeared to be just warming up. Music from an untuned piano plinked out a window that was cracked open an inch. Squeals and laughter spilled out as well.

Trace wasn't sure what crouching in the shadows beside the porch would reveal, but he bent his ear, listening.

Nothing came through the window crack, but it did through the front door.

Mrs. O'Hara's burly protector, Sims, held the subject of Trace's investigation by his shirt collar so that the toes of his shoes scraped the porch. He gave the skinny man a shake, then a toss.

The thin man landed bottom-first in the street, a tangle of long legs and awkward arms.

"We don't take to your sort around here, Perryman," Sims barked. He slammed the door.

Lantern light swayed back and forth across the man getting up from the dirt.

Trace had discovered some things, after all. One, the man's name was Perryman. Two, he wasn't even fit for a brothel. Three, he was a physical weakling. But four, he was all the more vicious because of it.

The swing of light across Perryman's face showed him smiling at the closed, and probably now locked, door. The next shift of light revealed him snarling, with unnaturally sharp, yellow teeth grinding, top against bottom, back and forth.

After a moment, he clenched his fists, turned and

growled as he walked away. Growled not like a dog, or even a wolf, but like a threatened cat, a sick cougar.

Cooper had been right—the man was creepy. What, if anything, could he want with young Jess? Possibly it wasn't Jess he was interested in; maybe he wanted to devour the poor feline.

In any case, Perryman needed watching.

Trace let him get a good distance ahead before he stood up from his hiding place. He followed him, hugging shadows and watching from behind trees.

Hell and damn! Perryman was taking a back trail through the woods that led to Hanispree.

With the children asleep in their beds and the fire banked low, Lilleth stepped onto her front porch and closed the door behind her.

The night was black, deep with shadows and secrets. There was one secret that would give itself up tonight: Lilleth would find a way to get to her sister. She might not get close enough to attempt a rescue, but she would figure a way to go about it.

She stepped off the porch and walked through the woods veering off on a trail that split from the path to town. She had never been frightened of the night before. As a child she'd run free in the moonlight, as an adult she entertained audiences by lamplight.

This night, though, was deep, cold and silent. The only sound was the wind scratching bare branches together, with a rasp here and a crack there. If a person believed in the other world, she might see a ghost slip past a tree or a goblin pop up from behind a fallen log to bare his wicked teeth.

Luckily, Lilleth Preston did not believe in those things. If she did she would have been forced to take the wide, level road to Hanispree. Since she could not risk being seen, she took the back road that her landlord had mentioned. She suspected that the timid man's ears still rang with the lecture she had given him on honesty.

He had been forthright about the trail that twisted through the woods. By day it was easy walking, but by night it was brimming with shadows and imagined threats.

She stepped quickly, anxious to be off the path. Even without supernatural beings spying from the shrubbery, the night air was snapping cold. The wind's icy fingers continually yanked back the hood of her cloak. After half a mile she gave up on keeping it in place and used her hands to clasp the front of her cloak closed.

"Who-o-o—" A sudden rush of cold air pushed from behind.

"Who-o-o yourself, you old wind."

One time she imagined she heard footsteps to her left, just off the path. When she looked all she spotted was a bramble bush ticking against a tree.

She hurried down the path, careful not to peer too closely behind trees or fallen logs.

At last she spotted Hanispree. The huge building appeared, then vanished beyond a dense growth of bare-branched cottonwoods. In only a few hundred more yards she would be out of the woods and onto the main road.

All of a sudden, she heard footsteps again. No spectral shuffle, no lithe-footed gremlin; this was a very distinct crunch of boots on the path...following her.

Very well, then. She hadn't spent her life avoiding the lecherous groping of men to simply be caught in the woods.

"Oh! Ouch!" she exclaimed, sounding helpless, injured. She bent over and grasped her ankle with both hands. "My foot!"

Crunch, step, crunch, silence. A shift of fabric warned her that the man was at her back and reaching forward.

By the saints, this was too easy. The idiot had presented her with a perfect target.

She clasped her fingers together, forming one big fist, and in the same instant locked her elbows. She spun about. Swinging upward, she landed a blow to the man's throat.

"Ugh!" He toppled backward, landing in a prickly bush. The miscreant grasped his neck, gasping for breath.

"Why you…you great—" She drew back her boot, aiming for every man's tender spot. "Clark?"

"Ugh!"

"Clark!" She dropped to her knees beside him. "Are you hurt?"

"Yes." His voice sounded it, all raspy and raw. She helped ease him to a sitting position, then plucked a burr from his jacket.

"Well, you were about to get hurt a whole lot worse." She loosened his fingers from his throat and looked at the red welt she had left. "Just give it a minute or two. You'll be all right. What were you doing out here, anyway?"

"Protecting you." That sounded a bit better, a wheeze instead of a gasp.

"From what? Things that go bump in the night?"

"You were being followed." He stared at her oddly, while he rubbed his throat. She couldn't quite tell if the look was reproach or admiration. At least his voice was nearly normal now.

For an instant his remark about her being followed shook her. Not a soul knew she was coming out tonight. And Jess thought he had been watched the other day.

Still, anyone on the path might look like a stalker to a librarian.

"So, you just happened to be on this path at midnight, carrying your ax, and by chance, happened to be behind me. And saw someone else following me?" She shook her head. "Really, Clark, that seems a tall tale."

"Not tall enough." He stood up, yanking a sticker from his trousers. "Lilly, are you in some kind of trouble?"

"No, of course not!" This was a conversation she was not going to have.

"What are you doing out here at this time of night, then?"

"That was my question to you."

"Fair enough. I'll tell you what I'm doing if you tell me what you are doing." He stuck out his hand to confirm the deal with a handshake.

She accepted the shake. To be fair, it turned out to be less a shake than an embrace of hands. It lingered too long and his fingers caressed her wrist.

"You first," she said, to break the spell that might be once again ready to lead them to risky behavior.

He let go of her hand.

"I've noticed, when I deliver books, that on occasion the inmates of the hospital go without fires to warm their rooms. I'm on my way to light them."

Lilleth glanced at the cold, dark windows of the huge building. Was poor Bethany shivering inside even as they stood outside? Worry made Lilleth's stomach sag within her.

"How often is 'on occasion,' Clark?"

"As far as I can tell, nightly." He turned and retrieved his ax from the ground. "Your turn."

"You, Clark Clarkly, are a very good man."

"I hope you're not trying to flatter your way out of your confession."

"There's really not much to confess. I couldn't sleep." That was the truth. She'd barely had a solid night's slumber since Bethany had been incarcerated. "I went for a walk."

He squinted at her. Well, here was something odd. Clark was not wearing his glasses, and yet he seemed to be seeing just fine.

"Just for the record, Lilly, I know you are making that up." He swung the ax over his shoulder. "Come on, I'll walk you home."

"You most certainly will not!" And she was not the only person making things up. She would keep quiet about those missing glasses and just see if he bumped into anything. "I'd never live with myself if those poor folks inside froze while you walked me home."

"You can't walk all that way alone."

"That may be, but I'm not going home. I'm going with you."

This was the most unbelievable luck. When she'd stepped out of the cabin she hadn't dreamed that she might actually get inside the mental hospital.

"They say it's haunted," he warned.

"They say that someday we won't need horses to pull our wagons." Lilleth looked him in the eye, hard. She pointed her finger past him toward the hospital.

"I'm going in that building with you, Clark Clarkly, and that is that."

To prove her point she turned on her heel and walked toward it. For a moment she didn't hear his footsteps following. She did feel his gaze frowning at her back.

"Suit yourself, then," he said, catching up in a few long strides. "Just make sure you keep quiet."

"You'll hardly know I'm there."

So far, Trace found Lilleth to be true to her word, and useful in the bargain.

She was careful not to speak above a whisper. She helped him carry wood. She smiled at the inmates, fawned over them and charmed them. When the ancient Mrs. Murphy would not believe that Lilleth was not Trace's ghostly bride and the reward for his good deeds, she simply patted the old woman's hand and thanked her for her good wishes.

After he had warmed the last hearth, and motioned toward the door to leave, Lilleth tugged on his sleeve.

"That can't be all of them?" She glanced at the closed doors up and down the hall. "Are you sure we haven't missed someone?"

She tapped her foot…one, two, three.

"What's wrong, Lilly?"

"What could be wrong?" Her foot tapped faster. "I

think we might have missed someone, is all. What's up those stairs?"

"A bolted door."

At once she ran for the steps, lifted her skirt and dashed up them two at a time.

"Lils, what's going on?" She didn't hear him; he'd known she wouldn't in her haste to reach the door at the end of that long dark hallway.

When he caught up with her, she had reached the door and pressed her ear to it.

"If someone's in here they're going to be cold as stone."

He prayed that no one was in that room, but instinct told him there was. He'd never heard a cry or a plea for help, even though he'd pounded on the door.

"Let's go. It's late," he said.

Trace walked down the hall, even though he sensed that Lilleth hadn't followed. He stopped with one foot poised over the first stair heading down.

From down that long, dark hall came the most beautiful voice he had ever heard.

He pivoted about and saw Lilleth leaning against that closed door…singing a lullaby. Even at this distance he saw tears shimmering in her eyes.

He opened his mouth to warn her that someone might hear. But then, a ghost could sing a lullaby as well as anyone. He let her finish, then walked back down the hall and turned her away from the door.

"Why were you singing? What's going on?"

"There could be someone trapped inside." She wiped her eyes on her coat sleeve. "I thought a song might help."

"Come on, let's go." He slipped his arm about her shoulder and she let him lead her out of the building. He closed the door and picked up his ax from beside the woodpile.

She huddled under his arm, allowing him to hug her close to his side all through the sleeping woods, along the winding path.

There was more going on than she was admitting. He ached to ask her what it was, but she wouldn't tell him. He knew that for a fact.

So they walked in silence, leaning into each other until they reached the cabin's front steps. By then her tears had dried to frozen, salty tracks.

Tiptoeing up two stairs, she turned and faced him eye to eye.

"Will you come for Thanksgiving dinner?" she asked.

"Yes."

She went up the rest of the steps. She turned and sent him a subdued smile before she slipped inside and closed the door. He heard the lock shift into place, then jiggle as though she was checking its security.

He wondered at what point she would remember that she couldn't cook.

Chapter Eight

"Auntie Lils, you've got flour on your nose." Jess scanned her powdery appearance, hair ribbon to boot toe. "And your elbow."

"I'm well aware of that, young man, but biscuits don't magically appear on the table."

"They used to, back home."

Jess ducked when she flicked a pinch of flour at his nose.

"Back home you had someone trained in the art of biscuit making to set them before you."

"I never saw Mrs. Farmer with white stuff all over her...and the kitchen."

Lilleth scanned the cooking area of the cabin's main room. White dust covered nearly every surface. The only reason Mary wasn't covered in flour was that she was ten feet away, tied to a chair at the dining table, merrily banging a tin cup on the wood planks.

"I don't suppose you ever saw Mrs. Farmer dip her fist, fingers and all, like this." Lilleth smeared her hand in the heap of flour on the small table beside the oven, where she'd set out the mixing bowl, eggs and lard. "I don't suppose she ever did—"

Lilleth lunged, patting her hand on Jess's small rump. "This!"

The boy squealed. He dashed for the biscuit bowl and scooped out a fistful of his own.

He was quick. Lilleth didn't have time to dodge the white cloud coming at her face.

She blinked through powdery eyelashes, then wiped her face with both fists.

Jess doubled over, laughing. Bethany would want that. It's why Lilleth had begun the biscuit fight, even though her own heart was weighted with worry.

"You look like a raccoon, Auntie!" he said, trying to catch his breath.

"And you look like you got a—"

A loud knock sounded at the front door.

"That's Clark! Come to help me catch the cat." Jess dashed in that direction.

"Don't you dare open that door!" she called after him.

Oh, mercy, all powdered in white, she looked like Clark's ghost bride.

Jess opened the door wide. Clark stepped inside, pushed along by a gust of wind.

He straightened his glasses, peering wide-eyed at

her through the lenses. How interesting that today he needed them.

"Good day, Clark." She tried to straighten the blue bow binding the loose hair at her nape, but it was hopeless.

"Lilly?"

Blame it, half a smile tweaked his lips. She must look incompetent to the bone.

Her plan had been to impress him with her new-found skills, not make him laugh. Which he was doing, and quite hardily, even if he did manage to keep it inside.

"Ma's practicing biscuits," Jess announced, while he grabbed his coat off a peg by the door. "She'll be better at it by Thanksgiving."

"Oh, without a doubt. Let's go get your cat."

Jess dashed out the door.

Clark followed, but before he closed the door behind him he turned.

He winked!

"Well!" She slammed her hands on her hips, smiling in spite of herself. "This will be the tastiest Thanksgiving dinner that Mr. Clark Clarkly has ever eaten, mark my words, little Mary."

She had three days to make it so. Seventy-two hours to go from novice to queen of the kitchen.

Snow was on the way, hard and heavy. She'd heard the prediction while she walked down the boardwalk. Not by speaking with anyone about it, naturally. The fewer people she socialized with, the safer it would be.

In passing, she'd caught a word here and a sentence there, enough from each conversation to know that, along with the turkey, the good folks of River-walk might have a blizzard for Thanksgiving.

Lilleth stepped into the mercantile, grateful for the stove in the middle of the floor that invited icy shoppers to warm their backsides. This afternoon, she was the only person warming herself at the grate.

With only one more day until Thanksgiving, she had expected a crowd.

Lilleth stretched her gloves toward the fire. She skimmed her mental list of things she needed to purchase. Somehow those things would come together to provide a feast. Other women cooked; they did it daily. Blamed if she wouldn't do it, as well. It was simply a matter of mixing flour, and such, then there you had it. Somehow.

She put away wondering about the mysteries of gravy when thoughts of Clark crept into her mind. The man was perplexing, fascinating even. What was it about him that had tugged at her since the very first time she'd met him?

And what kind devilment had gotten into her, inviting him for a feast cooked by her own hands?

He made her feel safe, was what.

Had it not been for the pit of lies and deceit that

she lived and breathed on a daily basis, she would have asked him not to take the short walk home the other night.

Clark was the kindest, most decent man she had ever met. And honest on top of all that. In case those things were not enough, she wanted him in a most carnal way. Somehow, the librarian had gotten under her skin, burrowed himself into her heart.

Her bedroom walls were thick, made of solid logs, and the children were sound sleepers. Had life been different, she would have invited him for more than dinner.

She'd never met a man she wanted in that way. It could be because she'd never met a man she completely trusted.

She trusted Clark.

Walking home from Hanispree, tucked under the shelter of his arm, she had wept against his chest and found sanctuary.

Even though that moment of refuge felt good and right, she was not entirely comfortable with it. Being her own guardian had served her quite nicely her whole adult life.

In the end, she could not deny that having someone watch out for her gave her that extra bit of courage.

Right now she needed courage. Clark believed that someone had been trailing her in the woods, at midnight no less. All afternoon while she shopped in town, she had felt creepy crawlies itching between her shoulder blades, just as Jess had described.

She was surer than ever that he hadn't imagined he was being spied on the other day.

Thank the stars that she had come to town alone today and left the children in the warm safety of the cabin. The cabin with the sturdy lock that Clark had insisted on installing with his own, not so bookish hands.

Lilleth shook off a shiver. No one was watching. Her nerves were getting the best of her, what with the pressure of cooking a holiday feast. Not a feast for just the children and Clark, either; she'd make enough food for all the folks locked up in Hanispree. *I'll find you, Bethany.* She sent the thought for the thousandth time.

The mercantile owner came out from behind the curtain of the storeroom, wiping his hands on his long apron.

"What can I do for you, missus? Hope you don't want a turkey—sold out of those yesterday. Folks came in early, stocking up for the storm. No one wanted to get caught without a bird for Thanksgiving."

Luckily, she didn't need a bird. Clark was supplying that, although she would still need to cook it. From what she had been able to learn from the cookbooks that Jess had sneaked home from the lending library, turkey was the easiest part of the meal to fix.

"I don't need a turkey. Just some green beans, a dozen cans of milk." If a blizzard was coming she would need to have extra milk on hand. "Make that two dozen cans, along with potatoes and a big bag of flour."

"You go through all that flour you bought the other day already?"

"My biscuits are renowned." Hopefully, he didn't see her blush at her womanly failing to prepare the perfect bun. "I can't seem to make enough of them. They disappear almost before they are out of the oven."

That might be the case at some point in time, after she practiced a few dozen more batches. Hopefully, Jess wouldn't turn into a lump of dough for all the sampling he'd been doing.

"In fact, let me have two bags of flour. They are that good."

She laid money on the counter to pay for the food.

"You'll need help with all that. I'll send my boy over in the buggy."

"Thank you. Here's something for his trouble." She placed a quarter on top of the bills.

"You take care, Mrs. Gordon. That blizzard's going to be a killer." He scooped up the money and slid it in his apron pocket.

Lilleth turned to walk toward the front of the store. A man, his hat tugged so low it flopped over his ears and nearly hid his eyes, peered through the window. Ice crystals frosted the glass where he breathed on it. He grinned at her, then licked the pane with a long narrow tongue.

Just as quickly as he'd appeared, he vanished.

"Did you see that?" She spun about, but the mercantile owner had gone into the back room.

Had the apparition even been there? She'd like to hope that it was merely stress getting the better of her. Just in case, though, she'd ride home in the wagon with the storekeeper's son.

The turkey had nearly frozen while Trace went from the lending library to the cabin. So had he. The five minutes it normally took to walk that distance stretched to fifteen.

Wind howled past his ears, swirling snow every which way. He knew he was on the path only because he didn't bump into a tree.

Predictions of a blizzard had been underestimated. This storm was a violent force that breathed menace down turned-up collars, and foreboding up pant legs. Pity anyone who got caught out in it.

At least his family in Chicago wouldn't be expecting him to wire them his tardy progress report on the investigation.

A lamp glowing in the cabin window reassured him that he was going the right way. He leaned into the wind and pressed toward it.

The Gordons must have been for watching for

him. As soon as his frozen boot touched the porch the front door was flung open and Jess rushed out to take charge of the turkey.

"Ma thought you wouldn't come," he said. "But I knew you would, Clark."

The boy looked up at him, grinning. The gladness illuminating his eyes made Trace want to go down on his knees and embrace him.

It was plain to see that Jess missed having a father, one who would be around no matter what. Apparently, without meaning to, Trace had stepped into the role. He shouldn't have let that happen, but it had come about so naturally that he hadn't noticed until this instant.

Besides, this was Lilleth's son, her own flesh and blood. He could no more turn away from him than he could the boy's mother.

Jess crossed the room, carrying the bird to Lils. He almost staggered, tipped to one side with the weight of it. She lifted it from his arms, her face flushed from the fire she had just built up in the stove.

"Wait till you see my surprise, Clark!" Jess dashed toward his mother's bedroom and disappeared around the corner.

"He's been on pins all morning with excitement. I didn't expect you'd make it in this weather. You must be frozen through." Lilly brushed a spot of snow from his shoulder.

"It would take a worse storm than this one to keep me from this meal. I'd have crawled through the woods if I had to." He shrugged out of his coat, then hung it on a peg on the wall beside the fireplace.

Lilleth smiled at him, bright and pretty. Something about her was different today. She looked at him with softness in her eyes. Or maybe it was simply holiday cheer.

He'd give thanks today for that, even if what he should be giving thanks for was that she hadn't discovered who he really was.

Jess came around the corner, walking carefully and carrying a big cat in his arms.

"He finally came to me, just like you said he would." The boy's small chest seemed to puff up with pride while he carried his prize across the room. "Just in time, too."

As if to emphasize the point, a screeching wind grabbed hold of the cabin. It pounded, as though it wanted to blow the place down, but being made of good solid logs, with all the holes repaired, the structure held without a creak.

"He's a fine cat." Warmth from the fireplace on one end of the cabin and heat from the stove on the other chased the chill from Trace's clothes, then his bones.

He bent down to gaze closely at the cat, which purred with contentment in Jess's arms.

"Might be the finest I've ever seen." Trace stroked

the orange head and got a nudge in response. "Maybe he'd like some turkey, later."

"Bet he would. He's hungry as anything." Jess settled in one of the chairs beside the fireplace and snuggled the feline close. "He already gobbled down two eggs and four of Ma's practice biscuits."

"Those must be some good biscuits, then."

Jess arched a brow, then shook his head, long and slow. Luckily, Lilleth was busy sliding the turkey into the oven and didn't seem to notice.

"Where's your sister?"

"Napping." Jess bent his nose into the cat's fur and nuzzled.

Halfway between the kitchen and the fireplace, Lilleth had constructed a bedroom of sorts for the children. By stringing up blankets she had given them a private space near enough to the fire to catch its warmth.

Trace walked over to it. He drew back the curtain and peered inside.

Mary, sucking her thumb, snuggled in the small bed that he had given her. Red ringlets curled about her precious little ears. If the Thanksgiving ever came that he was giving thanks for a sweet baby daughter like this one, he would be a happy man.

"If you wake her up, it will be you who entertains her," Lilleth whispered, standing close beside him. Her breast grazed his arm ever so briefly when she peeked around him to look at Mary. "Why don't you

go sit by the fire, Clark? The turkey won't be finished cooking for hours."

"Can't I help with anything?"

"And you a guest? I should say not. Take yourself
over to that chair...put up your feet. They've got to
be frozen through." She nudged his arm, urging him
toward the fire.

He sat down beside Jess, kicked off his boots and
crossed his feet on the hearth to let his socks warm.
They talked about this and that while snow blew past
the window and the wind screeched and moaned
under the eaves.

Firelight cast the room in a warm amber glow.
Logs snapped, flames hissed and danced, burning
fresh sap. One log burned through, then crumbled
to a blanket of coals.

Trace added another one. At some point he fell
asleep. He couldn't have guessed how long he dozed,
but he woke to the sound of Lilleth singing softly
in the kitchen and the scent of the bird roasting in
the oven.

With the bottom of his socks toasty and his heart
simmering in a pot of contentment, he kept his eyes
closed to better listen to the voice that he had longed
for over too many lonely years.

If he could choose a moment of his life to last forever, it might be this one. Outside, the storm raged
like a banshee, but it also isolated this snug little
house from the rest of the world. He had a sense of

such peace that he doubted anything could intrude upon it.

"Mama...ba," said a small voice at his knee. "Tee."

He opened his eyes to see Mary staring up at him.

"Hello there, ladybug." With pretty red ringlets framing her face, she did look the part. He lifted her into his lap. "Did you have as good a nap as I did?"

She laughed and poked her finger in his mouth. He kissed it.

And that was how the afternoon went. Playing with the children, while he listened to Lilleth sing in the kitchen. Smelling the food while it cooked, and grinning, although maybe he shouldn't be, at the fact that this storm would probably keep him from returning home tonight.

Chapter Nine

Lilleth joined hands with Jess and Mary. Across the table from her, Clark did the same.

She closed her eyes and listened while he gave thanks for the food and the company, then asked for blessings upon distant family and friends.

"Amen," she murmured, praying for a loved one not so distant at all.

While they ate, she gave silent thanks for three more things.

One was that no one had gagged on her biscuits. Clark had eaten two of them, and while that may have been due to the good manners of a guest, Jess had gobbled down three. After enduring all her practicing, her nephew might have politely set one aside after the first bite. Perhaps her culinary future held more surprises than she might have dreamed.

Another was that Clark Clarkly had been thrown

into her life's path, perhaps by fate or by the spirit of her late brother-in-law.

Clark was not a dashing dandy of a man. Not the kind to make a woman's heart skip at the sight of him, and truly, she praised the heavens for it. Men like that, she had learned time and again, were not to be depended upon.

Clark was a good, upstanding librarian, a man that a woman could trust her heart to…and possibly even her secrets. Maybe Lilleth ought to consider telling him who she really was. Given what he was doing at Hanispree, he was in a position that he might be able to help her.

Then again, it had been said that silence was golden.

The last thing…and maybe she ought not to give thanks for something scandalous…was that the blizzard would prevent him from going home tonight.

She was very thankful for that, because even though Clark might not make most women swoon, he most certainly did it to her.

It made no sense. He made no sense. Men did not make her heart skip. More often than not they were cads who needed outwitting. Clark was as sincere and reliable as the printed word on a page.

Just here was where he made no sense. He was everything safe and yet…not. He was temptation and seduction sitting right across the dinner table from her.

Reliability didn't make knees weak and breasts long for touching. Trustworthiness did not turn a high-principled woman into one who sat across the Thanksgiving table from a man and lusted after him.

Who was Clark Clarkly, really? Now and again a feeling of familiarity passed between them in a glance or a word. For that instant it seemed that they had known each other in another lifetime, which was silly, since she did not believe in other lifetimes.

Still, when he laughed, as he was doing now at something that Mary had gurgled, it sounded like an echo.

"What is it, Lilly?" Clark asked, arching his brows and shoving his glasses up the bridge of his nose with one finger. "You look a thousand miles away."

"Pie," she answered, mentally drawing her attention back across those thousand miles. "It's pumpkin, but I purchased it from the bakery. Would you like it now or later?"

"I'd like some now *and* later, if it's no trouble."

"Me, too, Ma! Some now and some later, just like Clark!"

"Some now, and bedtime later," she declared, because that was what Bethany would say.

Jess took his time eating his pie, long enough for Mary to fall asleep in the crook of Clark's arm.

It was well past Jess's bedtime when he finally swallowed the last bite and patted his belly.

"Off to bed with you now, young man."

"But, Ma, I never got to discuss with Clark what to name my cat." Jess walked to the hearth and scooped up his feline.

"It might be that something will come to you while you sleep," Clark suggested. He stood up and carried Mary to Lilleth.

"Could be." Jess lugged his cat toward the blanket that partitioned off his room from the rest of the house. He lifted the flap. "We can discuss it at breakfast, then, since it's snowing too hard for you to go home."

Bless Jess for so innocently bringing up the subject that Lilleth didn't know how to, without a dozen inappropriate visions filling her mind.

Her nephew disappeared behind the curtain. She watched it fall, and felt Clark's hands brush hers, lingering a moment longer than would be required to pass Mary to her.

It wouldn't be wise to look up at him this very instant and risk him seeing her expression. If she didn't, though, she would not know what he was thinking.

She took a breath and glanced into his eyes.

"Please do stay," she managed to say quite politely, given that his thoughts very clearly had taken the same imprudent path that hers had. "It's far too dangerous to walk home."

"I appreciate the offer," he answered just as politely. "And I accept."

She hugged Mary close, then followed Jess behind the curtain.

Well-mannered words had disguised what was truly going on between them. She wanted him to touch her in all the ways a man touched a woman… her heart and her body. He wanted to touch her, but she knew he wouldn't.

A make-believe marriage stood between them. A man who didn't even exist kept her from knowing Clark more intimately than she had ever known anyone.

She laid Mary down in the little bed that Clark had given her, and kissed her curly head.

Kneeling beside his bed, Jess whispered a prayer for his mother, then hopped under the quilt and tugged it to his chin. Lilleth kissed his forehead, then stroked the cat.

She parted the blanket doorway and stepped into the main room.

Clark sat in front of the fireplace with his back to her and his stocking-clad toes pointed at the flames.

One thing was certain. She could not share her body without first sharing her secret.

Trace knew that he was a villain. Everything about him was a living, breathing lie. To let his Lils, a vulnerable, abandoned woman with two precious children, get caught in the deception that was Clark was unforgivable.

He glanced sideways at her where she sat in a chair beside him, watching red-hot logs crumble into coals.

She seemed distracted.

Telling her who he was would be the right and honorable thing to do. It would also betray his family. No one ever broke character in the middle of an assignment. Not for health, wealth or convenience... and most especially not because of wanting a woman.

So here he sat with a miracle beside him, nearly desperate for more than a kiss from her, and all the while he was being held hostage by Clark Clarkly. Not to mention her miserable husband who might even be dead.

The bedroom curtain rustled. Paws whispered across the floor. The cat, as orange as a pumpkin, brushed his chair then hopped onto the windowsill. He batted one paw at the snow blowing against it.

Beside Trace, Lilleth began to tap her foot.

He turned in his chair, set his feet on the floor and looked her in the eye.

"Is something wrong, Lilly?"

"Why would you ask?" She stood up, walked to the kitchen and a moment later returned, bringing him a slice of pie.

"You're troubled. Tell me why."

"Well, there's all those hungry people shivering away their Thanksgiving at the mental hospital, while we sit here warm and full, for one thing." She paced to the window and stared out, stroking the cat's back in a distracted manner.

Those cold and hungry people bothered him, as well, but there was nothing to be done about it in a blizzard.

"I think it's more than that. Are you worried about your husband?"

"Hardly." She glanced at him and rolled her eyes.

A wave of relief swirled through his belly, further proof that Trace was a villain.

"Talk to me, Lilly. Tell me what's wrong."

"Very well," she said, her blue eyes crinkled in a frown. "I like you, Clark."

"I like you, too."

She shook her head. A lush mane of red curls shivered down her back.

"That's the problem." She opened her hands, palms up. "You can't like me. You don't even know who I am."

"I know who you are."

"You only think you do. The fact is…I'm not Lilly Gordon. I even hate the name Lilly."

"What should I call you then?" Lils…and nothing else would do.

"Lilleth. Lilleth Preston."

"Was that your maiden name?" he asked, pretending to be startled at her revelation.

"Not was, Clark. Is." She wrung her hands in front

of her. "I've never been married. Until lately I've spent my nights singing with a traveling show."

"But the children?" Good Lord! What kind of horrors had she endured, raising Jess and Mary out of wedlock?

Lils tipped her chin up a notch. She took a breath and stared down at him where he sat like a sorrowful lump on his chair.

"Close your mouth, Clark. Unmarried women have children more often than you might imagine. But the truth is that Mary and Jess are not mine. They're my sister's children."

He stood up slowly because the blood had suddenly drained from his head.

No detestable husband? She wasn't a mother? The perfect little girl had grown up to be a liar?

"Why tell me now?" He was surprised that his brain and his tongue could work despite the shock.

"I'm in some trouble. I think you are the only one in a position to help me."

This was where he ought to wrap himself up in righteous indignation and storm out of her house. She had lied to him, outright and bold. What else was there her about her that he didn't know? She could be a criminal, or had she grown up to be like her mother, a woman of easy virtue?

"I'm so sorry, Clark." She hurried away from the window and knelt in front his chair, looking up into his eyes. "I don't suppose a man like you would know anything about being dishonest. But the children's safety was at stake and in the beginning you were a stranger. Please forgive me."

He wanted to crawl in a deep hole and cover himself with dirt. Forgive her? The only difference between them was that he was a worse liar than she was. She at least had the decency to finally admit the truth.

He did not.

If he blurted out now that she was his long-lost love, she would hate him. He wouldn't blame her.

And if she hated him she would not allow him to help her out of whatever trouble she and the children were in.

Just as on the day he had knocked her over on the train platform, he was stuck being Clark Clarkly.

A tear glistened at the corner of her eye. Lils never gave in to weeping, so he let that tear tremble on her eyelash without wiping it away with his thumb.

"What is it? Ask me anything."

It might take time away from his investigation, but family be hanged, he was going to help.

"I'm breaking someone out of the mental asylum. I need your help."

He hadn't expected that. To break an inmate out of the hospital wouldn't postpone his investigation, it would ruin it. The place would be locked up so tight after that he'd never learn another dirty detail.

He'd be the first son to be dismissed from the family business. The rule not to become personally involved in a case was taken so seriously that it might have been the eleventh commandment. Already he'd crossed the line by taking care of the inmates.

He'd be exposed. He was stuck on a high wire with no way down.

"Who?" he asked, and sounded like an owl more than un intelligent human.

"My sister, Bethany."

It was odd. The Bethany he remembered was as sound of mind as anyone.

The tear at the corner of Lilleth's eye slipped down her cheek and broke his heart. He would do anything for her.

It meant continuing to live as Clarkly. But he knew this as well as he knew Clark would stumble when he stood up…Lilleth thought he was an honest man, and if she found out he wasn't she would not accept his help.

Here it went, blast it. He sat down on the floor beside her.

"Tell me everything."

"Bethany's husband passed away six months ago and left her a fortune. His twin brother, Alden, figured the inheritance ought to have been his, so he locked my sister up." Lilleth shook her head and pushed a wispy curl away from her cheek. "He believes that by controlling her children he can make her give him whatever he asks. Since he owns the place, there's no one to tell him no."

One more horror to be noted when Trace wrote his exposé. How many more victims were there like Bethany?

"Before you say yes…or no, Clark, you should know that I'm a criminal. Alden is the children's guardian. I kidnapped them."

He didn't know what to do. He had to help Lilleth. Innocent children were in danger.

Still, he couldn't sacrifice all the inmates in order to save one. The mental hospital was no more than a prison. It was his job to write about it, expose it and have it shut down.

For the first time in his life, Trace honestly did not know what to do. He felt half-sick at his options.

A log crumbled to coals in the hearth, sizzling and popping. The cat stood up on the windowsill and growled. It arched its back, a ridge of orange fur peaking along its spine.

Lilleth rose and hurried to the window. She snatched the cat to her chest and peered out at the blowing white.

Trace reached the window in two long strides, placing her firmly behind him.

Anything might spook a cat, most likely the crumbling log in the fireplace. But it could be a vile bug eater that spooked this one.

There was no longer any doubt that the man had been spying on Jess.

Just in case the fool was crazy enough to be skulking about in the storm, Trace yanked the heavy curtain over the window. He reached out and tugged at the lock on the front door to make certain it held fast.

Lilleth carried the cat back into the children's bedroom. A moment later she came out and went to the kitchen area, silently wiping the stove down with a damp rag.

"I saw a man in town," Trace said, watching her hair sway with her scrubbing.

She dedicated her attention to a stubborn spot and attacked it. The fabric of her skirt shimmied over her hips.

"He was watching Jess," he said.

She dropped the rag and turned to face him, her hands braced on the countertop behind her. "Jess noticed him." Her expression was tense. "I believe he was leering at me through the window of the general store yesterday, too."

"His name is Perryman. Alden's spy, he has to be. He was following you in the woods the other night." Trace would take care of the spy. That was one thing he knew he would do.

She moved away from the counter, crossed the room and stood before him.

"I'm trusting you to keep my secret, even if you can't help me. Please say that you will."

"You can trust me with your life, Lilleth."

"I thought as much," she murmured, and touched his wrist when he folded his arms across his chest. "I knew you would be a friend that very first day, when you took us in."

"Anyone would have." He needed to step back, not take her shoulders in his hands.

"No one else did. There's something about you." Her eyes held his. "I can't explain it, and surely I sound like a ninny, but you make me feel like...like I've been waiting for you forever."

Had she waited? He had no right to expect her to have. He had no right to ask.

"Have you been?"

"I don't know." Her brow crinkled. "What is it that people wait for, Clark? Not what men gave my mother, not what one gave me behind the—"

He crushed her mouth with a kiss, and half a second later all he cared about was the press of her plush breasts against his chest.

He whispered "Lilleth" in her ear, but Lils in his heart. He kissed her again, this time slowly savoring her and afraid that if he lifted his mouth she might reveal what that cad had given her.

"Well," she murmured at last, when he found the courage to allow her a breath. "He didn't give me that."

"I can't claim to be sorry."

"You've just made it clear to me that in some ways

I'm still a virgin." She curled her fingers into his shirt. "Come with me into the bedroom, Clark."

"The children?" He nodded toward the blanket wall.

"Sleep like rocks." She smiled up at him. "Even when I try to wake them, I can't."

"You mean a great deal to me, Lilleth. I think you should know that."

She let go of his shirt, took his hand and tugged on it. "Come along, Clark. I intend to mean a great deal more."

Firmly, resolutely, he dumped the voices of his parents, his siblings and his own nagging conscience into a deep mental well in his brain. He covered it with a lid.

Whether Lils was put in his path by a remarkable twist of circumstance or something more marvelous, here she was. He could no more turn away from her than he could the obligation he had cast into the bottom of his moral well.

He picked Lils up in his arms and carried her into her solid-walled little bedroom.

Chapter Ten

Lilleth had never been one to believe that blood could hum. Or if it could, it was a dull and dirty tune.

And yet notes that she had never known existed trilled through her.

She tried to sing them, which made Clark nuzzle her neck and quicken his pace.

"You sound like an angel, Lilleth," he whispered against her neck. He set her down, but slowly, so that her belly slid over his hips and his…my word, but a man's anatomy could go through some remarkable changes.

"I don't feel like an angel." She leaned across the bed to light the lamp on the night table. She turned the wick low, then straightened and reached behind Clark to close the door. "I feel rather wicked."

Amber light flickered over his face. It lapped his shoulders and caressed his thighs where he stood at the foot of her bed. The bedroom was a small space, which made him seem taller, broader in the chest and more virile than any male she had ever met.

Something curious had come over her. This fanciful yearning for a man was a thing she had never expected to experience. Flighty women felt fanciful, not her. But there was no denying the fact that she wanted to be the lamplight, kissing the line of Clark's cheek and stroking the curve of his lips.

Now, being well past the age of blushing maidenhood, she did just that. She reached up and felt the masculine shape of his jaw and the scrape of beard stubble under her fingertips. She pressed her thumb to his lips and traced his smile.

"You've never had a wicked day in your life," he murmured against her flesh.

"You only just found out who I really am." She lifted the glasses from his nose and set them beside the lamp. "You can't possibly know that."

"I told you…I know who you are." He touched her hair and cupped the back of her head in his hand.

The gold flecks in his eyes seemed to swim in the blue, which had to be a trick of the bedside lamp.

"We've known each other such a short time," she said. An old shadow began to take shape in her mind, then drifted away like a ghost.

He shook his head. "We were in love, a very long time ago."

He didn't know her, not really, but for this one night she would allow fancy thinking because she felt fancy…and dreamy, with a connection to this man she could not explain.

"You read too many books, Clark, but it's a sweet game…pretending once upon a time." She sighed and closed her eyes. "What were we like way back when?"

"So young that falling in love was the most innocent thing in the world." She felt him kiss her cheek, and smelled his warm breath close to her mouth.

Suddenly the fabric of her dress felt heavy, the air in her lungs too thick to breathe. Clark pressed her palm over his heart. Beneath the woven cotton, it thumped against her fingertips.

Clark took a step back. She opened her eyes.

He reached for his glasses, but she plucked them up from the nightstand and hid them behind her back.

"I have secrets, too, Lilleth. Secrets that I have to keep."

"Everyone has secrets." Whatever they were, they couldn't be as awful as hers were. It was unlikely that he was a kidnapper.

"I'll sleep in the other room."

She shook her head and reached her free hand toward him. There was so much about life that she didn't know. At her age, she ought to know.

"Clark, show me why grown men cry when I sing a love song."

He gripped her fingers, then sat down beside her on the bed.

He turned her face toward him, grazing her cheeks with his thumbs. He stroked her hair from root to tip, pausing for a moment over her breast. Her heart danced like a whirligig under her ribs. She wondered if he felt it against his knuckles.

"They cry for things that used to be. For things they can never get back."

He kissed her sweetly before he stood up and walked backward three steps, looking perfectly miserable.

"Good night, Lilleth," he whispered, then went out.

"Stars shine bright," she murmured to the closed door.

The ghost in her mind took the shape of a boy for the space of one heartbeat.

"Good night, Trace," she whispered, then rolled onto to her side and turned off the lamp.

Trace opened the cabin door and stepped outside. Snow swirled in circles.

He took a lantern with him down the stairs, scanning the ground for footprints. He breathed the cold air deep into his lungs. It stung, but that was nothing compared to the pain in his soul.

Everything he'd ever wanted had just been handed to him, and he'd turned his back on it for the sake of duty.

He didn't know if he'd be able to help Bethany.

For one thing, she might be in that room with the mammoth lock. Truthfully, the way the weather had been lately, and denied the warmth of a fire, would she have survived? He'd never heard even a whimper coming out of the cell, even though he'd called through the door.

The frightening truth was that it might be too late for Bethany.

The one thing he could do was take care of the spy.

He lifted the lantern and looked again.

Nothing. Any footsteps that might have been left behind by a prowler had been filled in with snow.

Back on the porch, Trace swiped the snow from his face, brushed it from his shoulders. He went back inside and bolted the door.

He didn't think it likely, but there might be a prowler with the stamina of a polar bear.

He dumped another log on the fire, then sat down on the hearth with his rump toward the flames.

He tapped his fingers on his knees and wondered what Lilleth was wearing on the other side of the bedroom door.

He stood up when his backside grew hot. He strode to the window and drew back the curtain to watch the snow fall. After a few moments, the cat hopped up on the ledge, pacing and turning, and drawing its tail across his shirt.

"I reckon you need to go out." The cat nudged his

palm with its head. "Not a chance of that, sport, for you or for me."

The cat purred, so he carried it to the chair in front of the hearth.

Trace settled into it. He ought to be used to spending the night in chairs by now. One would think the wood wouldn't feel so hard on the bum.

With a stretch and a flex of its claws, the cat snagged the weave of his pants. Then, with a flip, it offered up its furry belly for stroking.

"You've never been in love, have you? You don't look miserable enough."

"Clark, wake up," Lilleth whispered. A feminine hand shook his shoulder.

Trace cracked his eyes open a slit.

His back ached. When he had decided to sleep on the children's bedroom floor the wood hadn't seemed as hard as it did now.

The cat, which had been sleeping blissfully on Trace's belly, stood up, stretching and arching. He leaped off and strode out of the blanket room, tail swishing.

"I'm going out." Lilleth leaned over Trace wearing a heavy coat and a furry hat. She clutched a canvas bag to her chest that was clearly stuffed with food.

He struggled to his elbows and groaned. "Snow's too deep to go anywhere."

"Snowshoes." She lifted her foot and brought it

down on the floor with a clunk. "They were with all that junk in the back room."

"Snowshoes or not, it isn't safe to go out, even if the snow did let up."

"That may be, but I won't allow those poor people in the hospital to miss their Thanksgiving meal." She shook the bag at him.

It was difficult to argue with Lilleth while she was hovering over him. He stood up, stretching the stiffness from his muscles.

"I'm going with you."

"There's only the one pair of snowshoes. Besides, I was hoping you'd stay with the children. If there is someone lurking about…"

He had to admit, it wounded him that she could launch into a mercy mission so wholeheartedly only hours after the intimate moments they had shared last night. It was almost as though she had dismissed the kiss and the fact that they had come within a heartbeat of making love.

"I'll take care of Mary, Ma," Jess said, popping his head out from under his blanket. "I'll lock up good and tight after you leave."

"You can call me Auntie now, Jess. I told Clark all about us."

The boy sat up and blinked. "Are you going to help us get Ma out of that place, Clark? We've been wondering if my pa put you in our path so you would."

Lilleth tilted her head to the side, staring up at him. She arched her brows, echoing Jess's question.

He sat down on the bed beside Jess.

"Son, there's nothing I'd like better than to break into Hanispree and get your mother out. The fact is, I…well, there's—"

"Jess, Clark is a librarian," Lilleth said. "Breaking folks out of mental hospitals isn't what he is used to doing."

"But he knows lots of things."

"Well yes, that's true. Perhaps if he has read about a breakout, he can advise me on how to go about it."

All right, he deserved that unmanly observation of his skills, but it rankled.

"Give me your foot," he said to Lilleth.

She backed up a step, shaking her head, narrowing her gaze at him.

He grabbed her ankle, untied the rawhide lacings of one snowshoe and yanked it off. He did the same to the other.

"What do you think you are doing?" Lilleth bent to grab them back, but he strapped them to his own feet.

Since it would have been useless to tell the Lilleth of old to stay safely at home, he didn't tell the grown-up Lilleth to stay home, either.

"Come with me," he said, stuffing his arms into his coat, then buttoning it up.

He opened the front door and turned to see Lilleth staring doubtfully at the one and only pair of snowshoes. Turning around, he motioned for her to hop on his back, piggyback style.

"Last chance." There was something about watching her perplexed frown flash into a grin that made him want to laugh. Little Lils had accepted the call to adventure with that very same smile.

Holding the canvas bag in one hand, she dashed across the room and leaped upon his back. He hooked his arms under her knees and stepped outside. He turned to look at Jess, who appeared perfectly, delightfully, scandalized.

"Lock that door up good and tight, pal," Trace said, and then trotted down the steps.

He felt like a boy again, cavorting with his Lils. It was easier than he would have thought to let the years fall away and remember how it had been to be happy and innocently in love.

Lilleth pressed her nose into Clark's upturned collar. Even though the storm had passed, the weather remained bitterly cold. She took a deep breath, savoring the warmth, inhaling the scent of his skin where it permeated the wool.

Something had become perfectly clear during the half hour trek through the snow. Clark had not always been a librarian. To the casual observer he might appear clumsy, but nothing, she had come to discover, could be further from the truth.

A bookish man would not be able to carry a full-bodied woman and her bag of food all this way without wheezing and groaning. And for a man who claimed to be nearly blind without his spectacles, he hadn't tripped over a single fallen log.

She'd be a flat note in a perfect melody if he needed them at all. Just as soon as he pulled those glasses out of his breast pocket was when he would begin to stumble about.

It was as clear as the icicles hanging from the eaves of the mental hospital, just coming into view, that Clark Clarkly was not the man he portrayed himself to be.

He had claimed to have secrets, but she hadn't paid his confession much attention.

She'd been so caught up in wanting him that she hadn't noticed much else. Even now, when the heat had cooled and a new day begun, she still wanted him.

Clark was handsome and virile, everything a man ought to be…and she wanted him to be the one to teach her things she had always considered foolish. To show her why a woman would surrender good sense, lay it at a man's feet and be glad for it.

"It's such a beautiful building," she murmured, while Clark carried her past the big iron gate, held ajar by two feet of fresh snow. "It must cost Alden a good sum to keep up the appearance."

"Appearance is all this place is. At its core, it's ugly."

"I'm curious about something, Clark. How did you discover how awful this place is? I wouldn't think Hanispree's secrets are something that a librarian would just stumble upon."

"I'm nosy." He shrugged.

She adjusted her weight against him. While he might not be showing signs of stress, her legs were becoming tingly where they hooked through the crooks of his elbows. "Is it safe coming here in broad daylight?"

"It's not safe. But this was your choice, if you will recall." At the back door of the inmates' quarters, he set her down. "You were right, though, Lilleth. There's no telling how cold and hungry the people inside might be."

"Who are you, Clark?" She stared at him while she stomped the tingling out of her legs. A flicker… a shadow crossed his eyes. "Who are you really?"

He didn't answer. He turned the knob on the back door, but it was locked. Last time they had come it had not been. Walking inside had been as easy as entering her own front door.

"Follow me," Clark said. The snow under the eaves of the buildings was not too deep. She was able to walk over it without needing his help.

He pointed to a window a few feet above his head.

"We can get in this way if the sash isn't frozen to the frame. Can you stand on my shoulders?"

"I grew up freer than most boys." Clark looked away from her all of a sudden. Clearly, he didn't believe her. "Stoop down."

She stepped on his shoulders, crouched, then braced her gloves on the wall.

"Okay, stand up slowly." She climbed the wall with her hands, stretching taller as he elevated her. She and Bethany had used this trick on a few occasions.

Level with the window, she tried to slide it open. "It won't budge."

"We'll have to try and jar it loose."

She hit it with her fist, but it held firm.

"How's your balance?" he called up.

"Better than yours."

She thought she heard a curse, but she must have misheard. This was Clark, after all.

His shoulders shifted. She held on to the window frame. A moment later he handed her a snowshoe.

It took a few whacks, but she freed the window and shoved it open. She scrambled inside, then looked back. Clark reached up to give her the bag and the other snowshoe and then jumped, gripped the sill with his fingers and pulled himself up and inside.

Very interesting, she noted. It took a good bit of strength to do that. Most men wouldn't have managed it.

He went to the back door and leaned the snow-shoes against it. If anyone came in that way they would clatter to the floor.

Very clever, Clark. You are more than you seem. Her thoughts came up short when she heard a voice.

"Everyone is cold, Mrs. Murphy." The speaker sounded edgy…more than impatient.

"We wouldn't be if you'd use the fireplace for its intended purpose, Nurse Fry."

"Hush your mouth, you old hag. Be grateful that you aren't out in the snow."

"I'll be grateful when I pass to my Maker and leave your nasty personage behind."

"Those belligerent words will get you tied to your bed without your breakfast."

"For all the good that will do you." Mrs. Murphy's aged voice crackled in laughter. "The ghost will set me free the moment you leave here."

"You've done it now. It's the ropes for you."

Bedclothes rustled. The old woman tried to stifle a grunt.

"You are a bully, Miss Fry. The ghosts don't take kindly to bullies."

"Ghosts? So there's more than one now?" Nurse Fry snorted in derision.

"Why yes, the specter has got himself a brand-new bride. A pretty thing, too, and so kind."

"It's no wonder you're locked up in here, you crazy old loon."

"In my time, I was as sane as you are, and prettier by far."

"I'm going to have to slap you for that. Insulting the staff is against the rules. Let your ghost friends help you now."

Clark lunged forward, but Lilleth touched his arm, stalling him and drawing him around the corner, where the stairwell led to what she feared to be Bethany's frigid cell.

She cupped her hands over her mouth and started to sing. Her voice trilled up the scale and down, sounding eerie as it echoed through her fingers. She held long high notes, then moaned over low ones.

Miss Fry screeched. Her heavy footsteps pounded down the hallway. The door to the pleasant part of Hanispree opened, then slammed closed. The key in the lock snapped, its echo whispering down the hallway.

Clark dashed ahead of Lilleth into Mrs. Murphy's room. By the time she rushed in behind him, the frail woman was sitting upright with her bindings on the floor.

"You shouldn't anger the nurse, Mrs. Murphy," Clark told her.

"Oh, I feel quite safe having my say." She patted Clark's hand when he traced the red welt the rope had made on her arm. "I knew you were close by."

"But I might have been in another realm."

"Oh, and there is your bride! What a lovely voice

you have, my dear. Please do sing again, but something more cheerful than the melody you sang the other night."

"I'll do that." Lilleth knelt beside Mrs. Murphy and arranged the thin nightgown across her shoulders. "I sang that one for my sister. She's locked up here. Her name is Bethany. Maybe you know something about her?"

"Would she be Mrs. Hanispree?"

Lilleth nodded, her voice trapped by the lump in her throat.

"Well, she'll need your help. I haven't seen her, mind you, but I do hear things."

"What do you hear, Mrs. Murphy?" Clark asked.

"That nasty doctor tries to get money from her. Every few days they take her out of her room for short periods of time. When they bring her back they are mad as hornets. I reckon she's not giving them any."

"Do they hurt her, do you think?" Clark covered Mrs. Murphy's knees with a thin blanket.

Panic cramped Lilleth's stomach while the woman appeared to consider her answer.

"Not as far as I can tell. Her spirit doesn't sound broken yet." Mrs. Murphy touched a strand of Lilleth's hair that curled out from under her fur cap. "I used to have pretty hair. Maybe I will again when I pass over. That's something to look forward to."

"Thank you, Mrs. Murphy, for telling me about Bethany. What can I sing for you?"

"Something that I can tap my toe to, if you please. In my time I could dance with the best of them. My dance card was always full." A distant smile crinkled her lips. She appeared to look inward, perhaps watching that lively girl whirl once more about the dance floor with a dozen hopeful beaux looking on. With a blink and a sigh, she returned to her cold, dark room. "And dear, for Mrs. King in the next room, perhaps a lullaby. Sometimes I hear her talking to a baby. The poor thing doesn't guess it's only her pillow."

For nearly an hour Lilleth went from room to room, singing, while Clark passed out food and warmed cold hearths.

The last door she stood before was Bethany's. Just as before, it had a special lock that looked impossible to breach. No food for her sister, no warmth for yet another night.

"The children are safe. I've got them tucked away in a cabin in the woods not far from here." Lilleth spoke quietly, digging her fingers into the dirty, splintered door. "Don't give up, Bethany. I'll get you out of here."

Something in the room hit the floor with a thud. It shattered. No doubt her sister was tied and gagged, with no way of communicating but that. Only a heavy door and a miserable lock separated them.

It was enough to make Lilleth want to scream in despair.

She didn't, though. She didn't even whimper, because Bethany needed to know that everything was under control, that there was a plan to set her free.

"I hear you." She pressed her forehead to the wood and stifled her grief. "I'll be back for you, just as soon as I can."

Clark touched her shoulder and drew her away from the door. He supported her down the creaky stairs.

She sniffled into his coat collar while he carried her on his back through the icy woods, all the way to the cabin door.

He set her down on the first step of the porch and cupped her cheeks in his hands.

"Please excuse me, Clark. I'm not a weeper, not usually."

He wiped a smear of icy tears from under her eyes. He kissed her cheek, grazed her lips, then kissed her other cheek.

"What would you say if I told you that you might be the woman I've always dreamed of?"

Without waiting for her answer, he turned and sprinted down the path toward the lending library.

Chapter Eleven

She would have told Clark that dreams were all well and good. They were the stock and trade of librarians, after all.

Just now, leaning back against the front door, she watched him tromp homeward over snow that glistened in the cold morning sunshine. The brilliance nearly blinded her eyes, but not her common sense.

This man was not a librarian, not in the usual sense, at least. Further, she did not want to be the object of his dreams. She wanted to be the object under his fingers, under his lips. What she wanted was to know him through and through, and for him to know her.

All of a sudden the door opened. A pair of fists grabbed the back of her coat and yanked her inside.

"Don't stand out there, Auntie." Jess slammed the door and shoved the bolt in place. "He'll see you!"

"Clark has seen me for the past two days," she

said, wandering to the window and lifting the curtain to watch him disappear around the bend in the path.

"Not Clark." Jess yanked the curtain closed. "The man in the outhouse."

Lilleth gripped Jess by the shoulders, staring down at him.

"Are you certain there's a man in there? You haven't gone out, have you?" She tapped her boot toe on the floor.

"Didn't need to, Auntie. Until you and Clark walked up he was hollering and thumping against the door."

"Serves him right, getting trapped in the privy." She lifted the curtain again and watched the outhouse. Even from fifty feet away she saw an eye peering out of the moon-shaped cutout in the wood. It might be days before the snow that had accumulated in front of the door melted enough for him to get free. "I suppose I'll have to let him out."

"He's the one who was watching me that day. It has to be him. Don't go out, Auntie Lilleth, he's probably dangerous!"

"Considering where he got himself stuck, I don't believe he's overly bright." She dropped the curtain.

"I'll go for Clark." Jess reached for his jacket.

"You most certainly will not, young man." She cupped his face with gloves that were still crusted with ice from her trek home perched on Clark's back. Worried eyes blinked at her. They looked equally like his mother's and his father's. "I'd let that miserable wretch freeze before I'd allow you to risk yourself in the cold."

"You might get hurt."

"Don't you worry." She ruffled his hair and wiped the frown from his forehead. "Your mama and I have been outwitting mean, stupid men from the time we could crawl."

"I can help."

"Well, naturally, I'll be depending on you." She tugged at her gloves and flexed her fingers. "First, go check on Mary to be sure she's still sleeping, then stand by the window and watch. If anything goes wrong, take your sister out the back door and run for Clark."

While Jess checked on Mary, Lilleth got a shovel and a rope from the back porch. She wrapped the rope around the shovel's handle, then gripped it in both hands.

She grinned at Jess to show him that he didn't need to be afraid.

She was, though. Over the years she'd learned that a woman needed that edge to keep the upper hand. Have confidence, but never underestimate your opponent.

Jess grinned back at her, and she was certain he was also hiding his fear.

She went outside and closed the door behind her.

"Lock the door, Abigail," she called loudly, going down the front steps.

The outhouse was fifty very long steps from the cabin. Snow nearly reached her knees. She high-stepped and struggled every inch of the way to the little wood building.

Wind whispered in the treetops and a beating of bird wings ruffled the air. Only silence came from the outhouse now. The eye no longer peeked from the moon-shaped cutout.

No doubt the moron planned to rush out at her, a helpless woman, and take her by surprise.

At least she hoped that was what he planned.

"Oh, my word, this trek to the privy is exhausting! Soon as the ground thaws I'm going to have my husband move it closer to the house." She stopped to wipe her brow and appear winded in case Alden's minion might be spying on her through the moon. "Next time my four little girls need to visit the privy, he is the one who will carry them all this way."

She rested her hand on her breast to make sure the man had time to plan his assault on her helpless self.

At the outhouse door, she began to shovel the snow away.

"All this shoveling is too difficult for poor little me. I may just squat right here in the snow, then holler for Harvey to come out and carry me back."

With most of the snow cleared away, she removed the rope from the handle of the shovel. She glanced up to make sure the eye was not watching while she wound the rope about the outhouse and across the top step. She tied a knot, good and tight.

"Only another minute until I have this door free. I doubt if it will be soon enough, though."

In fact, the door was completely clear. She took a few seconds to strike a helpless pose, while gripping the shovel behind her back.

Thirty seconds later the door burst open and the same face that had been leering at her through the mercantile window glared at her, blue lips snarling and teeth chattering.

He lunged and she stepped to the right. One of his shoes snagged the rope. He toppled. She swung the shovel and walloped the back of his head before he hit the ground.

Sprawled, with arms and legs pointing north, south, east and west, he lifted his head. She whacked it again, but not hard to do enough to do lasting harm. He would need some strength to stumble back to town, after all.

And really, had she wanted to kill him she would not have gone to this trouble. She would have simply left him in the privy to freeze.

"Harvey! Come quick," she called. "There's a stranger in the outhouse!"

She poked the shovel at his nose, while making sure to stay well out of his reach, just in case he was not as dazed as he appeared.

"You'd best not have been planning harm to me or my little girls, stranger." She walked backward toward the cabin with the weapon in front her, at the ready. "If I were you, I'd run away quick before Harvey comes out. My man is half bear and half cougar, and he eats strangers for breakfast."

She backed up the stairs and across the porch. The door opened behind her and she stepped inside.

Jess slid the lock closed, then hugged his arms about her middle.

"I almost felt sorry for him, Auntie Lilleth." He squeezed hard. "We didn't need Clark at all."

Hopefully, Jess didn't notice her trembling. Alden's spy had been weak because he was so cold, but the rage boiling in his eyes had all but burned her.

The men she had dealt with in the past were greedy leches, but none of them had such an aura of malevolence about them.

Had she been able to convince him that she was not the person he had been looking for? That a woman with four little girls and a beast of a husband lived in this cabin?

Or would he wire Alden and report that he had found Bethany's children? Worse, was Alden here already?

They did need Clark, more than young Jess knew.

On occasion, Trace's pen got him into trouble. Luckily, a fact reported incorrectly could be easily revised, or apologized for in the next edition of the paper.

This morning, as he'd dropped Lilleth at her front door, the trouble had come from his mouth. He had blurted out the truth. Lilleth was the one he had waited for all his life.

Luckily, she couldn't have known what he really meant by that admission.

There was that part of him, though, that wished she had. That she would toss her arms about his neck and tell him she knew exactly who he was and that neither time nor distance had changed her love for him.

With slush soaking his boots, Clark marched through the twilight toward the cabin.

The day had warmed and melted much of the snow. Come dark, when the temperature froze again, he'd probably be able to slide all the way home on the ice.

He carried the snowshoes over one shoulder and a bag of meat pies from the hotel slung over the other. Chances were Lilleth had taken every bit of food from her pantry this morning to give to the inmates at Hanispree.

As soon as he rounded the bend in the path, the front door flew open and Jess rushed outside.

"You should have seen it, Clark!" The boy waved and shouted from the porch. "Uncle Alden's spy got caught in the outhouse and Auntie walloped him good!"

Fear cramped Trace's gut. A picture flashed through his mind—of a young Lils on the ground, a pair of ruffians hovering over her and intending to do her harm. The scar on his chest began to throb with the memory.

Lilleth stepped onto the porch with Mary riding her hip.

"You should have come for me," he said. Why would she, though? No doubt she considered bumbling Clark too inept to handle the situation.

Jess answered first. "Auntie wouldn't let me. Said she would let that no-good fellow freeze to death before she'd allow me out."

She should have let him freeze. The man could only be Perryman. Mrs. O'Hara was not all that discriminating about her customers. If the purpled-haired madam tossed him out, he must be as vile as he had seemed that night.

"The fellow was a dimwit," Lilleth told him while he came up the stairs. "Baby Mary could have ousted him with ease."

Young Lilleth had never asked for help in dealing with her mother's unprincipled men. There was no reason to think she would now.

It hardly seemed possible that he could love her more now than he did then, but he was a man of facts and this was a fact.

"I brought dinner, since you must have emptied the cabin of food this morning." Trace went inside and set the meat pies on the dining table.

"Nearly," she answered.

"Auntie made biscuits for lunch." Jess opened the bag and drew in a lungful of aroma. He sighed over it. "Not that they weren't grand, mind you."

The four of them sat at the table, Jess beside Trace, hip to hip, and Lilleth across, with Mary on her lap. They asked a blessing for those shut up in Hanispree before they ate.

During dinner, Jess recounted how his auntie, armed with only a shovel and pretending to be helpless, had made the villain flee.

Trace asked if she'd ever done any acting with the traveling troupe and she replied no, but she'd been exposed to actors long enough to learn a few things.

They spoke of this and that while the fire snapped and the full moon cast a beam of light through the window.

This might be his world if he told Lils the truth... and if she forgave him.

With the four of them snug and safe, life had never seemed so right. Villains might be cavorting on the streets of towns across the country, needing to be written about and exposed, but for this one night, in this peaceful cabin, he would put that away. Troubles would still be waiting tomorrow.

For tonight life was as he had only dreamed it could be.

In time, the fire grew low. The beam of the moonlight crept across the cabin floor and Mary fell asleep in Lilleth's arms. Jess yawned and stretched.

"It's off to bed with you, young man."

"But Auntie, I'm not tired."

"Nonetheless, it's bedtime." Lilleth stood up and Jess followed her into the blanket bedroom.

Trace added another log to the fire and stirred the coals.

If Lils invited him to her bed again tonight, would he be able to walk away? Not very likely. Alone together, it would only be a matter of seconds before clothes came off.

How would he explain the scar that cut an L across his chest? Even though it had been many years, she might recognize it.

"Have you ever been swimming at midnight, Clark?"

He looked away from the orange glow of the coals to see her walking toward him with a bright, mischievous smile on her face. She truly was an exceptionally beautiful woman with her full bosom, her tiny waist and that mane of red curls shimmering over her shoulders.

"A long time ago," he admitted. With her.

"I had a friend once." She reached her fingers toward the flames. "We used to do that."

"Is he the one you mentioned in your sleep?" Trace wanted to cover his shirt so she wouldn't see how his racing heart made the fabric shiver.

She nodded. "Can you believe that I still miss that boy? His name was Trace. For some reason I've been thinking of him more often lately."

She gazed into the flames. He was grateful that she did, because he wasn't sure how he would react if he saw the memory of the young man he had been in her eyes.

"We thought we'd marry one day."

"What happened to him?"

"I don't know." She sighed, shrugged and glanced up, spearing him with her gaze.

And there it was. He saw it in a blink. After all these years she still hurt over their separation. Then as quickly as he'd glimpsed that sadness, it vanished. She grinned.

"What do you say, Clark? We might not have a pond, but there's a slick of ice outside and a full moon."

"I say, first one to land on their bottom owes the other a favor."

"Challenge accepted." She dashed out the front door ahead of him, down the steps and onto a patch of snow that had melted and refrozen into a large, smile-shaped ice sheet.

"I have to warn you, Clark. I'm a wizard on skates."

Cold air nipped her cheeks and moonlight glinted in her hair. If he didn't know better he'd swear that the great bright ball in the night sky was laughing along with her.

"That may be, but we're not on skates." He slid across the ice on his shoes, windmilling his arms and spinning in a fancy circle. "I've had lots of practice walking on ice."

"That was impressive, I do have to admit."

Lilleth demonstrated her own abilities by lifting the hem of her skirt in one hand and reaching toward the stars with the other. She twirled about twice on one foot without falling.

He'd have to work to gain that favor.

"Copy this, then," he challenged, and ran three steps, then glided thirty feet.

He nearly fell at the end of his slide, but he caught the glint of victory in her smile and managed to keep himself upright.

Lilleth shrugged. "You don't walk that well on dry ground."

That stung! It was Trace competing in this game, not Clark. If he wanted to keep his secret, and he was beginning to wonder if he could, he would be forced to take a tumble...but not just yet.

"Let's see what you've got, Miss Preston."

This time she lifted her hem high, anchoring it in both elbows so that her stockings flashed white to her knees.

He'd never known Lils to allow maidenly modestly to stand between her and victory.

She ran four steps, looking like a fairy tiptoeing over the ice, then slid past him with a laugh.

He reached for her hand, intending to keep her from gaining more ground than he had. When his fingers closed around her wrist, she lost her balance. She went down with a screech and a flounce of lace and wool.

"That, my friend, was cheating," she announced, reaching one hand up to him for help.

"Down is down." He shook his head, happy for the victory, even though she was right about the cheating.

He clasped her cold palm to pull her up, but she yanked, catching him off guard. His shoes grappled for purchase. He thumped down beside her.

"Down is down," she echoed.

"You took the first fall."

"Only because you played unfairly. As I see it, we ought to grant each other favors."

"I'll have a song," he said, wanting a kiss.

"And I'll have a waltz in the moonlight."

"Agreed." He stood and helped her to her feet.

He took her in his arms. She looped her hands around his neck and clasped her fingers together. He slid half a step to the left and she followed, her ribs shifting under his fingertips. He guided her in a circle. As it turned out, this slow dance over the ice was not a waltz so much as a moving embrace.

She looked up at him with her eyes reflecting moon glow and his smile. An instant later he swore that she looked into him rather than at him. She must know who he was.

Slowly her hand slid from his neck to his chest. She had no way of knowing that her fingers traced the shape of a heart over his scar.

Then she sang for him. Her beautiful voice told the story of a love, long lost but never forgotten.

It was about the two of them, many sad, long years ago.

He dipped his head to her shoulder. To keep up the appearance of a dance, he spun them in another slow circle.

He knew why grown men cried when she sang a love song.

When she finished, he lifted his head from her shoulder, took her cheeks in his hands and brushed his lips across hers.

What he wanted was to delve into her mouth in a seduction that would end with him delving lower. What he wanted couldn't be.

Even if he did admit the truth, it wouldn't solve his problem. Lilleth would hate him. The deception that he had played upon her was beyond forgiveness.

"I want to know why that song brought a tear to your eye," she whispered.

"I loved a girl a long time ago. Your song reminded me of her."

"Tell me about her."

He couldn't help it; he looped a red curl about his finger and felt it wrap his calloused skin in a caress.

"She was just like you."

She was you!

Lils frowned. Starlight winked a crimson crown in her hair. A gentle breeze washed the air with the scent of crisp, cold cedar. "You ought to try and find her, Clark. I think you still care for her."

She was wrong about that. He didn't simply care for Lilleth. He loved her more now than he had years ago.

"I care for her very much."

The time had come to choose. His career and the poor folks at Hanispree? Or the woman who was bound to hate him regardless of what he decided?

Without warning, his foot caught in a bank of snow. He toppled, carrying Lilleth down with him.

He landed on top of her, but she didn't struggle to be free of his weight. She touched his hair and wiped a smattering of snow from it.

"You fell," she whispered. "I get another prize."

"I hope you want a kiss." He felt her breasts rise in a sigh against his chest.

She shook her head. His hopes were dashed.

"I want you, Clark…all of you."

"Do you know who I am?"

"You're not a librarian." She plucked the glasses from his nose and tossed them somewhere. "I know you don't need those."

Her breath touched his and spun to fog in the inches that separated him from the kiss he wanted.

"Close your eyes," he whispered, and she did. "Listen to me, to the sound of my voice. You know who I am."

He kissed her. He touched her throat and her waist, wanting to give her all that she wanted. But he had to give it as Trace, not Clark.

"Don't you know me, Lils?" he asked. "It's me... it's Trace."

Chapter Twelve

"**B**allentine?" She shoved at his chest and wriggled out from under him.

She knelt beside him, gazing down at the man lying in the snowdrift with his hair tumbled over his forehead in disarray. Slivers of ice clung to the dark tips and began to melt against his face.

This was not Trace Ballentine. He had disappeared into the mists of time. A boy cherished and hidden away in a secret, precious part of her heart.

This man looked nothing like her Trace. Her Trace had cheeks as smooth as her own. This was a grown man with hair on his face.

She peered hard at him while he pushed up on his elbows then sat up.

"It's me, Lils. It's Trace."

No, he was not. Trace had been slim. This man was lean, ripped with muscles. The boy had laughing, friendly eyes. This fellow stared at her, somber-eyed.

Something about his voice, though, made her listen closer instead of stomping on him where it would hurt the most.

Her Trace's voice had just begun to deepen when her mother had torn them heartlessly apart for the sake of her new, soiled love. But there was something…there in the tone. It was the same in the man and the boy.

"Say something," she demanded.

"Stars shine bright, sleep tight tonight."

Her heart slammed against her ribs. Blood throbbed in her ears.

"You might have heard me say that in my sleep."

"It's me, Lils." His gaze bored into her, clearly pleading with her to look back over the lost years and see him.

A rush of emotion flared in her chest, tightened her throat. It couldn't be true. This was impossible!

And yet it seemed that her lost love sat beside her with snow melting in his hair and dripping down his nose.

She stared into the face of a miracle and nothing short of it.

"Trace!" She tossed her arms about his neck and squeezed. "My Trace…" Now she began to sob. She felt like a little girl whose fairy king had returned. The boy had become— "Clark!"

Trace recoiled when she shouted in his ear. "That

fool doesn't exist." He reached for her, but she stood up and backed away. "I can explain if you'll let me."

"I will not. Not another word, you…you deceiver."

This stranger gazed up at her, pain clearly etched over his handsome features. "If I'd ever guessed I would run into you, there would have been no Clark," he declared.

Of course there had been a Clark. He had been as real to her as Trace had been. She had admired him…trusted him.

She had been ready to share her bed with him!

"Clearly, you are no longer the Trace I knew. That boy was honest and a good friend."

Or so she remembered. She'd thought the same of Clark, who was all of a sudden nobody.

"I think you are an impostor." She didn't, not really, but she wanted to.

"Do you want proof?"

"I certainly do not!"

But the stranger on the ground gave it to her anyway. He opened his shirt and exposed a scar in the shape of Trace's wound.

Words failed. She might deny who he was until she froze out here in the snow, and he would still be Trace Ballentine…or some form of him.

Not the one she had loved, though. Her Trace was dead and gone. Her Clark had never been.

What was she to do? She needed this man's help. Until a few moments ago she had wanted his love.

While she stood in the snowbank, stupidly gazing down, she thought of the girl she had been. Back then, she had always known what to do. She let the child in her out now.

She stooped and snagged a fistful of snow. She pounded it into a ball, then tossed it at the stranger's face as hard as she knew how.

He grimaced and shook his head. Beside his nose a red welt began to swell.

She hoped it turned black-and-blue by morning.

"Go back to your library, Mr. Ballentine." She gazed down her nose at him. "Or Mr. Clarkly, whoever you are at this particular moment."

With her heart feeling as heavy as the low note in a tragic song, she mounted the cabin steps.

She held her head high, though, while she lifted the soggy hem of her skirt.

Trace was not the only one who could put on an act. If she looked aloof and uncaring in the face of his confession, so be it. He didn't deserve to know to know how much he had hurt her.

Once inside, she shot the lock home, then tripped over to the fireplace, where she crumpled to her knees. She folded her arms on the hearth and buried her head in them. She wept, silently and bitterly, for the loss of her fairy king…and her librarian.

* * *

Alden Hanispree's collar grew tight. Anger pooled in his throat until he felt that he was choking on it.

He stood outside a rear window of the whorehouse, shivering in the night air. He would have come in the front door, but Willow would have charged him something. Thanks to Lilleth Preston, his bank account was not as big as a man like him deserved.

There was no sense in paying the madam for nothing, for the privilege of stepping on her carpet and looking at her girls as he passed.

The word was, Perryman had returned. He'd slunk back into town and had been hiding and whoring for two full days.

If he didn't need Perryman, Alden wouldn't hesitate to strangle him. That the fool could come straight here without reporting what he had learned was beyond maddening.

Alden pounded his fist on the icy windowpane. This wasn't the first time he had been left outside Slender Sadie's window waiting for Perryman to finish his business. She was the only whore who allowed the idiot to indulge in his favorite, disgusting vice.

"Open up, Perryman!"

"Not now," his voice grunted in reply.

"Don't make me break the glass."

Just as he'd figured, Slender Sadie's skinny hands

lifted the window. She wouldn't want the cost of the glass to come out of her pay.

Perryman sat at a table beside the window in his long johns, with Sadie sitting across from him. A crimson shift hung off the whore's shoulder revealing one small, sagging breast. A bowl of bugs, some dead and some still squirming, sat between them.

"Want one?" Perryman asked, retrieving a live worm from the bowl and sucking the slimy creature through his lips.

"What I want is to know if you found the brats."

"Don't know. Could be."

Alden breathed frigid air through his nose, but it didn't help cool his roiling temper.

Too enraptured by his feast to notice that he was about to be slammed by a blast of anger, Perryman licked his lips. He poked his squirming feast with one long, bony finger.

Sadie stood up, walked quickly to the door. Her hand shook when she went out and closed it behind her. Someone, at least, remembered the last time Alden had been unable to hold his temper in check.

He took three deep breaths. He couldn't afford to lose Perryman as an ally.

"Climb out the window and tell me what you know."

"I'll climb out once my balls warm through."

Not a soul on earth could rile him like Perryman could.

"I'll rip them off you and bury them in the ice if you don't tell me what you found out."

Perryman blinked his eerie-looking, coal-black eyes. "I found out that you don't hide in an outhouse if you want to keep your man-parts healthy."

Alden reached through the window and slapped Perryman's face. He couldn't help it. The only reason he regretted it was that now he'd have to have act snivelly and sorrowful or Perryman might close his mouth on any information he had gained. The man could be stubborn as a rock and just as dumb.

"I'm sorry," Alden grated through his teeth. "I appreciate that you were nearly unmanned. Please sit inside where it's warm while I stand out here and freeze my balls off."

"Nothing to keep you from crawling through the window."

Nothing but a revolting bowl of bugs, an idiot, and a fee he didn't feel he ought to pay. He clenched his fingers into fists and shivered. "Please...do tell me what you found out."

"I saw a lady, figured she was the one, since she had the kid and the baby with her. I followed her home one night, but then it snowed. That's when I got trapped in the latrine."

"It could happen to anyone," Alden lied.

"After all that, it turned out not to be her." He bit a dried roach in half. "When she came out to do her business, it was some other lady. This one had a passel of little girls and a big husband."

"How do you know that?"

"She said so, after she knocked me over with a shovel."

"Did you see the girls? Did the husband come out when she discovered a stranger in her outhouse?"

"Only thing I was seeing were stars from when she walloped me. If I'd been myself I'd have given her what for and left the remains for her husband to scrape off the snow."

Idiot! Idiot! Idiot! Alden bit his lips to keep from shouting it out loud.

"From what I've heard of Lilleth Preston, she can get the better of a man. No need to feel too bad about it."

"This woman weren't her. She had a voice like sand."

"Only one way to make sure." This was the very last thing Alden wanted to do, but maybe he could handle it if he wasn't alone. "I'm going to Riverwalk to see for myself, and you are coming with me."

"I'm staying here."

"Remember what I said? When we get my brother's money we'll buy this place."

Perryman's head snapped around. He got up to investigate something crawling in the corner.

"Don't mind things the way they are," he said. "Sadie let me eat bugs off of her—"

"I'll give you the singer," Alden said quickly. He truly didn't want to know about the insects. "I'll put her in the room with her sister. You can have them both. Eat bugs from between their toes, for all I care."

Perryman stood up and snatched his clothing from the floor. After he dressed, he folded his long frame through the window and stepped outside.

"Get me a warm room at the Riverwalk Hotel and it's a deal."

They would both stay in the hotel. There was no way Alden was going to go anywhere near his insane asylum.

Ghosts probably drifted over every inch of those grounds.

Three days had passed since Trace Ballentine's betrayal. Plenty of time to dry her eyes and decide that she did not need his help in rescuing Bethany.

She would do it on her own. That had been her plan from the beginning, after all. She hadn't spent all her life depending on herself only to rely on someone else to do something so important.

A great deal of heartache might have been avoided had she done so all along. She would still be Lilly Gordon and Trace would have remained Clark Clarkly, strangers who could bid each other good day and never give the other a second thought. Ships that pass in the night.

So here she was this fine sunny morning, sailing her lone ship up the steps of Hanispree Mental Hospital.

She opened the front door and walked up to a desk with a name plate on it reading Nurse Goodhew. A bored-looking woman glanced up at her.

Lilleth wondered what secrets she kept behind her indifferent gaze. Did she know about Bethany? Did she care?

"I'm here to see Mr. Alden Hanispree."

The nurse came to attention with a start. "He isn't here."

Lilleth glanced about the room, looking casually at this piece of art and that velvet chair, hoping that the nurse would not notice the relief that had to show on her face.

The room was a disgrace. Alden had to have spent a sinful amount of money on it, while those left in his care froze and starved.

She didn't want to think about the things that Trace might have uncovered about this place.

"That, Nurse, is quite impossible," she stated. "Mr. Hanispree and I have an appointment."

"You may call me Nurse Goodhew." She picked at a strand of her dark hair and glanced toward a side hallway.

"Very well, Nurse Goodhew, I'll wait by the fire for Mr. Hanispree. I do hope he won't delay me over-long."

"I don't believe you have an appointment. Mr. Hanispree rarely visits. What are you up to?"

With any luck the miserable creature would know soon enough.

"I beg your pardon?" Lilleth set her face in what she hoped was an incredulous look. "I have a signed contract. He is supposed to be here to pay me after I perform."

"Perform what?"

"Songs for the inmates, naturally." Lilleth opened her coat. She had put on a red satin gown—low cut, with glass jewels adorning it. It was the only professional gown she had brought with her when she'd come to Riverwalk. And only because a woman never knew when she might need to sing herself out of a situation. "Be sensible, Nurse Goodhew. Why would I come wearing this if I were not intending to perform?"

"Show me the contract."

Lilleth opened her reticule and withdrew the paper that she had forged last night. She showed it briefly to the nurse, then folded it neatly and put it back in the bag.

"Mr. Alden has agreed to pay me twenty dollars. In exchange I am to sing for each and every patient, one at a time."

"I don't believe you." Nurse Goodhew stood up. "Mr. Hanispree wouldn't hold with such nonsense. He certainly wouldn't pay for it."

"In any event, he isn't here to pay me my due." Lilleth sighed, shook her head. "I will perform an act of charity."

"Be on your way, miss, before I have you removed."

"I, Nurse Goodhew, will not be budged."

"Dr. Merlot!" she called. "I need some assistance."

A man strode into the lobby, looking well turned out, with a stethoscope about his neck. His eyes glittered brightly at the nurse, until he noticed Lilleth standing there in her red gown.

His glittering gaze settled on her, then sharpened in appreciation. Lilleth was well acquainted with the expression. Very clearly, his attention did not sit well with Nurse Goodhew.

"Dr. Merlot, this woman is a cheat and a charlatan. She wants twenty dollars to sing to the patients."

"I was offered twenty dollars by Mr. Hanispree himself. But since he has reneged, I have offered to perform as an act of charity."

"Thank you, miss, but no."

The doctor gripped her upper arm and propelled her to the front door. She felt a shove at her back and was suddenly on the outside, with the door locked behind her.

She had held out slim hope that singing would gain her entrance. Anyone who worked for Alden knew that he would not allow the inmates such a treat, that he would not want anyone to see their paltry living conditions.

Lilleth cursed and didn't care. She marched around the back of the building and stared up at the window Trace had hoisted her into. It seemed fifty feet up rather than nine…and it was closed. There was no way in.

She wanted to cry, but she wouldn't. She swallowed her tears and her pride and took the wide road to Riverwalk and Clark Clarkly's Private Lending Library.

Trace sat at his desk with his pen in his fingers, his mind blank.

His lone customer sat on the rug in front of the fireplace, reading and warming the chill from her young bones. Little Sarah never hesitated to venture out in search of a book, no matter how cold she got in doing so.

"What do you think, Mr. Clarkly?" She glanced up at him with freckles dotting her cute nose. The shadow of a frown crinkled her brow. His heart squeezed. "This one about the beautiful horse sounds good, but this other one about the drummer boy in the Civil War seems important. I can't decide."

"Don't decide. Take them both." The window rattled with a sudden gust of wind. "You'd better hurry home, miss. It looks like the weather might turn."

Sarah stood up. She slid her arms into her coat,

tugged on her hat, then scooped up the books and hugged them close to her heart.

"I'll bring them back real soon, Mr. Clarkly."

"Those are yours to keep."

Since he'd committed the cardinal sin of exposing his identity to an outsider, he didn't think Clark would be in business much longer. It couldn't hurt to give the books away at this point.

Even in the event that Lilleth did not expose him, his family was bound to find out. Keeping even a minor secret from a clan of sleuths was impossible. Each and every one of them knew each and every thing about the others.

Trace picked up his pen and stared at it. He could buy some time by doing one of two things. Number one, he could make up yet another story about why he hadn't reported his progress on the investigation. Or two, he could tell the truth…he had met a woman and revealed who he was. That might keep the family in an uproar for a day or two while they considered what to do about it.

He set the pen down and put the cork back in the ink bottle. A decision of this magnitude took more thought than he could give it with Sarah beaming at him.

"Truly?" The little girl's grin warmed the room more efficiently than the snapping fire. She stroked the leather spine of *Black Beauty*. "I'll take the best care of them forever."

The front door opened. Icy wind whooshed inside, along with an even icier looking Lilleth Preston.

Sarah dashed around the desk and hugged his neck. "Someday I want to be a librarian, just like you."

Lilleth folded her arms across her bosom. She rolled her eyes toward the ceiling.

"Good day, missus," Sarah said in greeting, and then hurried out the front door.

Trace stood up, hoping against the odds that Lilleth would rush into his arms. He had held on to a pin-size flicker of hope through the dragging hours of the night that she might have forgiven his deceit. That she had remembered the tender feelings they had once held dear between them.

He removed his glasses and set them beside the ink bottle, staring for a moment at the dark liquid under the label.

When he looked up, Lilleth's expression was neutral. She didn't appear angry, but she didn't appear warm. She seemed a stranger. They might have had no more history between them than a librarian and his customer.

"Mr. Ballentine." To his surprise, she addressed him without a shred of rancor in her voice. "I've come to ask something of you."

"Ask me anything, Lils." At least she was not shutting him completely out of her life.

"Two things, then." She tapped her toe one time,

then took a breath. "First, do not call me Lils. Second, I would like to hire you to free my sister from Hanispree."

"Hire me?" He locked his knees to keep from plopping down in his chair. "I would never take your money."

"You'll understand if I cannot accept a favor." Color rose in her cheeks, but her voice remained in stoic control. "After all, favors are performed between one friend and another. Even though you and I knew each other long ago, we are nothing more than acquaintances now."

He strode to the window and flipped over the sign from Open to Closed. He crossed the room to Lilleth in three long strides. He gripped her shoulders and stared into her eyes. Private thoughts remained secret behind her indifferent gaze.

After a moment she glanced away. He took her chin in his fingers, turning it up so that she had to look at him...to listen to him.

"I'll give you that," he admitted. "What was between us as children was a very long time ago. You probably forgot me."

She nodded her head and broke his heart.

"But this is now," he said. "What is between us has nothing to do with years ago. Casual acquaintances don't feel what we do when we kiss."

"I kissed Clark, not you."

Fair enough. He understood how she might feel that way.

He slid his free hand up her spine to the curve of her neck, then bent his lips to hers. To his relief she didn't bite him. To his joy she softened her mouth and leaned forward, close enough that the front of her coat grazed his shirt. He wanted to unbutton the heavy wool garment, to reach inside the bodice of her dress and show her that what they had had never gone away.

"Clark never kissed you," he murmured across her mouth. "It was always me."

"Who are you?" She pushed out of his embrace and strode to the fireplace, facing the flames. "Very clearly, you are not the friend that I remembered over the years."

"I've always been him. That night you disappeared, I didn't want to recover from my wound. But my mother cried, my father threatened. They were not about to let me slip quietly out of my misery. They pestered me until I had no choice but to get well. You've got to know—I never forgot you, Lilleth."

She seemed unmoved by his story. Still, she hadn't marched out the front door, so he continued to explain.

"Once I grew strong enough, my family moved to Chicago. My parents started a weekly newspaper that focused on exposing corruption. When we were of age, all us kids became involved. The paper prospered and became well-known. On occasion, we had to go undercover, and that meant taking on fictional identities. There was also an issue of safety since we made plenty of enemies along the way."

She glanced over her shoulder, then back to the flames. It took only that one peek to encourage him. Her countenance had softened toward him, if only a little.

"And what secret assignment are you on now? Are there villains running the hotel? Gouging guests and giving their rooms away? Or maybe the baker is using inferior products in his tasty creations? Tell me, Trace, what is so very important that you would deceive me?"

"The villains we are after are very real. Very dangerous."

"I suppose it must have something to do with unscrupulous landlords who lease splintering cabins to unsuspecting renters."

"Lilleth, it has to do with Hanispree. I've come to shut it down. To have the inmates moved to respectable facilities."

That made her spin about. She pointed her finger at him in accusation. "You will not move my sister to another institution, Mr. Ballentine!"

"No, I won't. I'll get her out of there."

And there it went, his career with the family gone. He should have known from the beginning that he could not turn his back on Lils. Even if she never forgave him, he didn't regret this decision.

She lowered her arm, but lifted her chin. "Very well, then. Come by the cabin this evening and we'll devise a plan."

What he needed was a plan for the rest of his life. He had just turned his future over to a woman who walked casually past him, bidding him goodbye with nothing more than a curt nod, while she dropped a hundred dollars on his desk.

"Take the money back or the deal is off."

She turned and plucked it up.

"I'll see you this evening, then."

Maintaining an attitude of indifference toward Trace was nearly impossible. In spite of everything, the very last thing Lilleth felt for him was indifference.

In a matter of minutes he would walk around the bend to the cabin. She still hadn't decided whether she wanted to dump fireplace ashes all over him or kiss him.

Preparing for his arrival, she had brushed her hair into a lovely coif, frowned at her reflection in the mirror, then ripped out the pins and fluffed the curls into a royal mess. Whichever way she wore her hair, it wasn't right. Too fancy made it look as though she was trying to cover the pain of his betrayal. Too messy made it look as though she was wallowing in it.

In the end she stuffed the unruly mass into a single braid. This was as poor a choice as the others had been, since stubborn ringlets popped out with every twist and tug.

With the children asleep, Lilleth stepped onto the front porch, a shawl drawn about her shoulders and a lantern gripped in her fingers. The beam cast its light as far as the top step of the porch. The path that trailed into the woods was invisible. She, on the other hand, was completely visible.

The prudent thing to do would be to go inside. Trace might not be the only one walking the trail on this moonless night. While there had been no sign of Alden's spy, that didn't mean he was not lurking, waiting to do the children harm.

Going back inside would be the wise thing to do, but at this very moment she needed the bite of the cold wind to rush about her. She breathed in deep, trying to settle on the side of anger or of forgiveness. As things stood now, she was dizzy from the constant tip of emotions.

Curse Trace for tossing her into this turmoil.

"Don't give up, Bethany," she whispered into the night. "I'm coming."

"You shouldn't be standing in the open like that, Lils." Trace's voice shot out of the darkness.

An instant later his boots creaked on the stairs and he stepped into the lantern's circle of light.

Kiss or kill?

"I'm no longer Lils, and I was perfectly safe on my own front porch." She strode into the cabin ahead of him.

"Better to be careful, though. Perryman might have left town, but if he did you can bet he went straight to his boss." Trace placed a burlap bag in her hands. "Apple pie. It was warm a few moments ago."

She removed the pie from the bag and set it on the fireplace hearth to heat.

Clearly, she could not kiss or kill until they had discussed how they would free Bethany. The pie would help keep her mind on business and off her long-lost friend.

She watched him place his coat on a peg near the door. He was tall, his shoulders broad, and his hips… that was something to consider another time.

He turned to smile at her and all of a sudden she saw years fall away. Without the librarian to confuse her, she recognized Trace. She tried to fight it, but memories and old feelings bubbled to the surface.

That one man could cause such upheaval to a woman's heart was beyond distressing. For an instant, she understood her mother.

She would never be like her mother, though. Understanding and making the same mistakes were far from the same thing.

With the pie and her guest finally warmed through, she brought a pair of plates and forks from the kitchen area. She set them on the dining table along with a knife that glittered in the softly glowing lamplight. She sat down, then motioned for Trace to sit across from her.

She watched the pulse in his throat tap against his skin.

"I reckon you'd like to use that knife on me," he said.

To her mortification, she would rather feel that throbbing bit of flesh under her lips. When she was young she had dreamed of a lifetime of sweet, tender kisses from Trace. Just now, the kisses she tried so hard not to imagine were not sweet or tender, but wild and wanton.

"If you have a plan to free my sister, I'll wait."

She sliced a piece of apple pie for each of them.

After they ate Trace got up and walked to the wall peg where his coat hung. He reached in the pocket, then returned with a short saw. He set it on the table.

"This is your plan?" She picked it up and turned it this way and that in the light.

"And what would you do?" He closed his hand around hers on the saw handle. She ought to have yanked free, but his fingers felt warm, strong and slightly calloused. She ought to have known he wasn't a librarian.

"I'd pick the lock." She set the saw on the table

with his hand still covering hers. "It would be quicker and much quieter. Please don't touch me."

Lifting one finger at a time, he released her hand.

"I've tried to. That one can't be picked." He shook his head. "All I can do is hope to cut it off."

"Let's go, then." She stood up and swatted her fuzzy braid from her shoulder to her back.

"I'm going alone."

She marched to the peg, plucked down her coat, then shoved her arms inside. "If you remember me as well as you claim to, you know that I will not be left behind."

"You wouldn't be my Lils if I could make you stay home safe and warm."

It would be good to wipe the hopeful smile off his face with a well-deserved slap, but the truth was, she wanted to see that smile. More than see it, she wanted to kiss it.

"I am not your Lils."

She walked into the cold, windy night before he could read in her expression that just maybe she was.

Chapter Thirteen

Lilleth stood in the open doorway of what she had believed was Bethany's cell. Trace stood behind her, holding the lantern high.

The room was empty. Not a bed or a blanket indicated that anyone had ever been incarcerated here.

"Not even dust to leave footprints," Trace observed.

"I know Bethany was here." Lilleth squeezed her eyes shut.

She would not weep. Fainthearted women came to sorry ends. Her sister would not come to a sorry end. Lilleth would not allow it.

She stepped inside the room, while Trace hoisted the lantern behind her. He carried it to each dim corner while she knelt on the floor looking for… anything.

"They won't have harmed her, Lils." Trace knelt beside her and placed his big solid hand on her shoulder.

Apparently he was not going to give up calling her that pet name, and just now she didn't have the heart to argue the point.

She would not tell him so, but at this very moment it felt good to be his Lils, to know that his strength was there to bolster her.

A loose shutter banged against the side of the building in the wind. Even though the gust didn't penetrate the thick wall, cold radiated from the stone as though it were a block of ice. Wherever they had taken Bethany, it must be warmer than this.

"Not all clues are seen," Trace said, standing and drawing her up with a hand under her elbow. "Let's pay Mrs. Murphy a visit."

Trace took off his shoes and indicated that Lilleth should do the same. She nodded in understanding and bent to untie the laces. To Mrs. Murphy they were ghosts who could drift about unheard.

In the unlikely event that a fainthearted caregiver was working at this time of night, spectral silence would be crucial.

Trace turned the lantern wick to low. His face took on an eerie glow. Hers would appear just as frightening. They must look like visitors from the underworld.

Lilleth opened Mrs. Murphy's door. The old woman sat on her bed, gazing out the window, but turned when she heard the squeal of the hinge. She gave them a crinkled smile.

"I was watching you just now. I didn't know spirits would have to walk all the way across the yard. I thought you could pop in and out at will."

"We can do that," Trace answered, while he squatted in front of the fireplace to stir life into the embers of the weak blaze. He placed a log on top and watched while it kindled to life. "But my bride and I enjoy a stroll after dark now and then."

"How lovely to be newly wed." Mrs. Murphy's smile turned inward.

Lilleth sat down on the bed beside her. "We have become concerned about my sister. She is not in her room and it's been swept bare. Did you hear anything? Any little thing that might help us find where they've taken her?"

The old woman's gaze shifted, her attention returning to the reality of the dank cell she lived in.

"Oh, yes, dearie. I did hear something." Mrs. Murphy looked at her with clear, sharp eyes. Lilleth was sorry to have yanked her from her vision of happier days, but it couldn't be helped. "It was the doctor. He came himself this time, and only an hour ago. He and Mrs. Goodhew both. I remarked to myself that it was odd. They never come here after dark."

"Did they say anything? Any little detail that might tell us where they took her?" Trace asked, still poking at the log.

"If they did, I couldn't hear it. Mrs. Hanispree was raising quite a fuss."

Lilleth thought she might be sick. A struggle meant that Bethany could have been harmed.

"Did it sound like they hurt her?" she asked through her tightening throat.

"Don't you worry about that, missus," Mrs. Murphy said, patting Lilleth's hand. "What I heard was the doctor grunt and Nurse Goodhew screech. Mrs. Hanispree got the best of them, she did."

"Maybe she escaped on her own?" Lilleth said hopefully to Trace, who was now standing and peeking his head around the doorway into the corridor.

"I doubt that," he said, glancing back inside. "This place is a fortress."

"That's certainly true." Mrs. Murphy shrugged. "The only ones who come and go freely are the ones who have passed on, like you two lovely young shades."

"They won't hurt her, Lils. They can't afford to."

"If you call me that one more time I won't be responsible for what I might do!" she snapped, letting her frustration take aim at him. He had to stop this. It was difficult enough to be near the man without him trying to resurrect her affection by calling her Lils.

Mrs. Murphy's hand flew to her mouth. "Do lovers spat even on the other side? I was so hoping things would be different there, being a place of goodness and love."

Lilleth felt terrible. Mrs. Murphy looked forward

to her journey to the other side with such optimism. It was heartless to dash the frail woman's hopes in order to express her own annoyance.

"Oh, it *is* a place of love," she explained quickly, and patted her hand. "But even there we are human, and sometimes harsh words are spoken. You needn't worry, though—lovers always kiss and make up."

"That's a relief." Mrs. Murphy smiled brightly at her, then at Trace. "Go ahead, then, kiss and make up."

"Well, no, not right—"

Before she could protest, Trace stepped forward and drew her up from beside Mrs. Murphy. He braced his arm around her back and tugged her close.

Since there was no way out of this situation without disillusioning the dear old woman, Lilleth lifted her face to allow one chaste, dry kiss.

She ought to have known that would be impossible. This was Trace, and she was, despite the intervening years, his Lils.

She should have pushed away when she felt the first flash of heat roar through her veins. That would have been proper. It would have been wise. But this was the kiss she had imagined forever…her fantasy flaring to red-hot life.

Mrs. Murphy would have no worries about a cold hereafter now.

Dawn came with heavy clouds breathing down on the earth. Clark sat at his desk and dipped his pen in the ink bottle.

This time, words would not fail him. The telegram to his parents would be short and to the point. Finally, with his feelings settled, his goal determined, he knew what to write.

Lilleth had kissed him. She had kissed him as Trace, not as Clark. In that instant his world had shifted and fallen into place.

Afterward, just as he had expected, she fought what she was so clearly feeling. On the way home through the woods she had seemed as icy as the frozen tree limbs they walked beneath.

Even so, he couldn't help but sit at his desk grinning at his pen. His imagination flared to life, picturing the ways that he would thaw her. In the end she would be his Lils again. He wrote with a firm, bold hand.

Mother…Father, cannot complete assignment. Have become personally involved. Have broken character. Understand that this will end my career.
Always, your son,
Trace
Postscript: Marrying Lilleth Preston.

That last would be a shock. Over the years he had been encouraged by one family member or another to forget her. The past was the past and best forgotten, they would preach. That would have been sound advice for most people, but it was different for him. His memory was such that he remembered things most people forgot.

He recalled that little girl in detail. He saw the spark of mischief in her smile, and even today he clearly heard her giggling laugh in his head. What his family could never understand was that the scar of their separation would be with him forever, not just the one on his chest.

With his decision finally made, Trace stood up with a stretch and a grin. He put on his coat and went outside.

One block into the two-block trek to the post office, it started to snow. He caught a drifting flake on his tongue.

He enjoyed the stab of cold on his flesh. It felt fresh, just as life did right now.

It was true that challenges lay ahead of him, but he was not without hope.

Lilleth had kissed him.

He struggled to adjust the weight of the alphabetically layered books in the crook of his arm, because that was what Clark would do, and he couldn't put the character away just yet. He strode, less than sure-footedly, the last block to the telegraph office.

He sent his wire without the angst he'd thought would go along with such a life-changing decision. Just because he quit the family business, something that no one else had ever done, did not mean that his life would be empty.

Just then, the reason that his life would not be empty stepped out of the bakery. Lilleth was bundled against the blustery day in a heavy coat. The wind nipped her cheeks with a pink blush. A few red locks streamed out from under her hat, to bounce and frolic about her face.

Only a thoroughly smitten man would think poetic thoughts of frolicking red curls. If she glanced up and saw him, would she be thinking poetic thoughts, as well?

He stood beside the telegraph office door and watched to see.

Coming out of the bakery, Lilleth shivered even under her heavy coat. She would have attempted to make flapjacks for the children's breakfast—they were kin to biscuits, after all—but her thoughts were distracted in so many ways she barely knew how to feel.

She'd lain awake most of the night trying to gather her thoughts into some kind of order.

First, where was Bethany? Lilleth would scream in frustration if she could. Where once there had been only a wood door and a very impressive lock keeping her from her sister, now she did not know where she was. Lilleth prayed one more time that Trace had been right when he said that Alden could not afford to hurt her. That she had been stashed in a fancy room at the asylum that was used to trick families into believing their loved ones were being luxuriously cared for.

Lilleth only hoped that someone had laid a fire in Bethany's hearth just as Trace had done for each of the inmates last night, before the two of them made the brisk walk home.

One more thing that left her sleepless was that the inmates were not the only ones to have had fires laid in their hearths. Trace had done a fine job of igniting one in hers.

Of all the wicked timing. She couldn't consider romance while her sister was in peril.

Even though, walking home, she had put on a brilliant show of iciness toward Trace, the truth was that his kiss had claimed her. It had nearly claimed poor Mrs. Murphy, too. The dear soul was looking forward to the other side more eagerly than ever before.

Lilleth couldn't afford to dwell on her feelings for Trace. But only a born and raised fool would deny that something life-altering had shot between them with that kiss.

Just in case this kettle of turmoil was not enough, she had Alden to consider. There was every chance that he was in Riverwalk. That could be the reason they had moved Bethany. Alden might have an apoplexy if he had to visit the inmate quarters.

Enough time had passed for that squirmy Perryman fellow to have reported to Alden about her and the children. Alden might be watching her from a window or an alley this very moment. The hotel was close to the bakery. She and her bag of quickly cooling pastries would be in full view of anyone caring to look.

All along, she had feared a visit from the marshal. Alden could have easily wired him and had her arrested at any time. Since he hadn't, it had to mean that he intended to deal with her in a more personal way.

She had met the man only a few times, but in private, Bethany had told her things about him. He was a wicked little man with filth in his heart. Greed was his core value.

With her husband alive, Bethany had had no need to fear him. He had simply been an unpleasant relative to be tolerated on holidays. In her grief, she hadn't recognized the danger he had become to her and the children.

Frowning, Lilleth glanced behind her at the boardwalk. On this side of the street no one had ventured out into the cold. But on the other side, she saw Trace standing in front of the telegraph office, grinning at her.

She glanced away with an insincere huff.

All of a sudden her heart tripped, stalled, then tripped again.

There was no one staring at her through the hotel

window because they were staring at her from the hotel porch.

Two doors down from where Clark stood, Alden Hanispree stared past Perryman's raised and wagging finger. He looked her in the eye and recognition flared.

It was too late to run. In any case, Perryman knew where to find her—where the children were at this very moment!

She returned their glares, stalling and frantically figuring out how to get the children away before the men could reach them.

She glanced at Trace for half a heartbeat, and in that second saw his expression harden.

He nodded back at her and all of a sudden Clark appeared.

She didn't stay long enough to see what he would do, but she knew. He would bumble his way down the boardwalk and no doubt bowl them over.

Even with his help, she might not have enough time.

She dashed around the back of the bakery, passed the library and ran up the trail that led through the woods to the cabin.

Maybe she would always love Clark Clarkly, just a little bit.

Lilleth raced toward the cabin, taking just a moment to glance at the path behind her. She prayed that

Trace had been able to keep Alden from following her. She would need ten minutes to get the children out of here and to the lending library.

The library was the logical place to go. It was the only place to go.

Every second mattered, because there was no other trail between here and there. She hiked up her skirt and ran with her head down, forcing her legs faster with each step.

She went down, hitting the frozen ground hard on her hands and knees. The impact jarred all her joints, but she forced the pain from her mind. Already the fall had cost her seconds that might change the fate of her family forever.

Still a hundred feet from the cabin, she began to yell, "Jess…Jess!"

When he opened the door, it was with a frying pan gripped in his fist.

"Put on your shoes and coat," she rasped, the harsh breathing nearly closing her throat. "Your uncle is on his way here."

"Holy cats!" Jess exclaimed, leaping away from the doorway as she charged through it.

She snatched Mary off the floor, where she had been playing with her rag doll.

Jess snagged his coat from its peg, shoving his arms inside while he ducked into the bedroom.

Lilleth stuffed Mary into her little jacket, then buttoned the baby up inside her own coat.

All the way home the wind had gained in intensity and the temperature had fallen.

She dashed to the kitchen, put the pretty Wedgwood baby bottle in her pocket, then hurried to the fireplace, where a line of clean diapers was strung to dry. She stuffed those in her other pocket.

"Let's go, Jess!" She stooped down and grabbed the rag doll off the floor, then put it inside her coat for Mary to hold.

Jess burst out of the blanket wall with his shoes on his feet, but not laced. Something squirmed under his coat. It meowed and poked its orange head from between the buttons.

He dashed past her toward the front door, not pausing as he reached down and scooped the skillet off the floor.

Once outside the cabin, Lilleth considered taking the children off the path and through the woods, where they would be unlikely to encounter Alden. That would take much longer, though, and they could become lost. With the first snowflakes of the storm already falling, she couldn't risk that.

Mary wailed, probably cold and hungry. Lilleth didn't try to quiet her. If she met Alden on the path, the baby's crying would make no difference.

"Run to the library!" she panted.

She was tired, and with the toddler's extra weight, Lilleth was slowing Jess down. Alone, he might be able to outrun Alden. At least one of the children would be safe.

"Clark will delay your uncle, but I don't know for how long."

"Clark?" Jess slowed his sprint to glance back at her. "Auntie, we could stop and have a picnic along the way."

That might be true. As Clark, Trace could bumble his way through anything…probably.

"Get along!"

Jess turned and dashed ahead of her.

Five minutes later she saw him where the path met the woods behind the library. He was coming back, dragging Trace's heavy ax on the ground behind him.

"Quick! Into the house." She plucked the tool from his hand.

He darted forward once more. While she walked backward, she cradled Mary under her coat and dragged the ax over dirty snow left over from the last storm. She did her best to obliterate their footprints.

It seemed a hundred years later that she reached the front porch and went through the door, which Jess had opened.

She said a silent prayer right there on the spot, a thousand times thankful that they had made it and that the door had been unlocked.

Jess put his cat down and took Mary from her arms. Lilleth hurried to lock the doors as the aches of the fall began to set in.

There was no fire in the hearth and she didn't dare light one. Both Alden and Perryman knew that the librarian was not at home. They were a pathetic pair, but evil-minded and cunning enough to notice smoke coming from a chimney with the librarian not there to light a fire.

Twelve long minutes later a key scratched in the lock and Trace opened the door.

Lilleth rushed to him and he hugged her tight about her shoulders. Jess wrapped his arms about the pair of them.

"I knew you'd come to me," Trace said.

She leaned into his strength. Just this once, it felt good to be able to depend on someone other than herself.

"Did Alden go to the cabin?"

He nodded.

"How did you hold him off for so long?" Jess asked, his voice brimming with excitement.

"Ah...well, it took a while for them to gain their balance." Trace grinned down at him. "Then they had to hold my books while I put them back in order. Turns out they didn't want to borrow any of them, however, even though I showed them picture after picture."

"I reckon I want to be a librarian when I grow up." Jess puffed out his slim chest. "One just like Clark."

"There might be an opening for that job." Trace

ruffled the boy's hair. "For now we've got to get you and your sister out of here."

"I don't know anyone in town we could turn to." Lilleth squeezed her eyes shut, thinking. She opened them and shook her head.

"They'll be safe with Mrs. Murphy," Trace said.

She began to object, but Trace shook his head, clearly set in his decision.

"Auntie..." Jess stood beside Trace, stretching as tall as he could. "Uncle Alden is that scared of ghosts. The last place he'll go is the mental hospital."

"What about the staff?" She wasn't convinced. "They might find the children."

"Maybe, but it's the best we can do. And it looks like another blizzard getting ready to blow. They won't stir from their own cozy fires."

"We'll be closer to Mama there, Auntie." Jess tugged on her sleeve, looking hopeful.

"I can't see that there's a choice, really," she admitted. Even though she didn't like having the children there, the asylum would probably be the safest place for them.

"Let's pack some food and get going. Hanispree might figure out that I was delaying him for a purpose. He could show up here."

Within moments they were rushing through the woods. Lilleth's palms burned, and so did her knees, but it helped that Trace carried Mary.

With half an ounce of luck, they would get to their destination before the heavy snow set in.

They did, but just barely. The walk back to town would be more of a challenge.

When they ushered the children into Mrs. Murphy's room, she clapped her knobbed and slender hands.

"Why, it's children! How I've missed seeing little ones." She motioned Jess forward. "Are you happy, young man? Even though you, too, have passed before your time?"

"Yes, ma'am, me and my sister both are happy as larks." He sat beside her on the bed. "We'd be obliged if we could spend some time with you, though. Our regular granny is busy on heavenly errands for a while."

Lilleth nearly gasped. She had been trying all the way here to figure out what to tell Mrs. Murphy. Her nephew was a clever little boy. Trace arched his brows and gave Jess an approving nod.

"That would be lovely." The elderly woman hugged Jess with a frail arm. "It's nice that you feel so warm and solid."

"That's one thing that surprised me about passing over." He leaned into her hug. "The warmth, even the cat's warm."

After an hour of settling in and seeing to the other inmates, Trace clutched Lilleth's hand and led her down the dark hall toward the back of the building.

She winced and he let go.

"I bruised them a little when I fell, is all." Near

the back door she stopped and glanced up the stairway. "Maybe they moved her back."

Trace shook his head. "I already checked."

"I'm scared, Trace." She didn't want to say those words. In a small way they admitted defeat.

"Don't worry—we'll find Bethany."

Snow fell in earnest now, blowing sideways and in circles.

"Maybe we ought to stay here."

"You can. Maybe you ought to tend to the children."

"What about you?"

"I need to be where I can see what Hanispree is up to. Chances are, he'll remain in town."

"I'm staying with you, then."

Lilleth breathed in the cold, fresh scent of ice and pines.

"Hold on to me, then, Lils. This is going to be some blower." Trace drew her in tighter.

"Say it again," she said.

"Hold on to me."

"Not that…"

Chapter Fourteen

"Lils?"

Maybe he had misheard, with the wind blowing in his ears.

"Lils," he repeated, trying the endearment out cautiously.

Wonder to beat all, she smiled at him. Even though her teeth chattered with the cold, there was no mistaking that she wanted him to use the forbidden name.

He'd like to take a moment to enjoy it, to consider what it meant, but the storm grew worse by the minute and her pretty lips shivered.

Too bad he didn't have time to kiss them warm and rosy. Evidence pointed to the fact that she might allow it.

"Let's get you back to the library before you freeze solid," he said.

"Alden and Perryman might find us there." He'd

never seen fear in Lilleth's eyes before and he didn't now. Still, the concern he read in them was not uncalled for.

"That pair of tenderfeet? The farthest they'll venture is the hearth in the hotel lobby."

Frost-tipped curls peeking out from under her fur cap nodded against his coat sleeve. She tried to walk at the urgent pace he set, but her skirt had become sodden to the knees and dragged like a weight behind her.

He scooped her up. It felt good to have her in his arms. To protect her. This was what he'd wanted from the first time he'd rescued her from a gossip's tongue, way back when.

Wind howled about his head. It blew his hat off. Snow stuck to his face and crusted his eyelashes.

"Almost home, Lils. There's the end of the path up ahead." He said it with more confidence than he felt. With the snow swirling from every direction at once, he couldn't be sure he was even on the trail.

"It's a lucky thing we got the children to Mrs. Murphy when we did." Lils's voice shook. He felt her shivering under her damp coat.

As numb as his lips were, he doubted that they looked as blue as hers did.

"I think I see the back door."

"Praise heaven…" Her teeth clacked.

He did praise heaven a moment later, coming inside and closing the door on the wind. He set Lils on her feet, then knelt beside the fireplace, piling on kindling and logs. He poked and prodded until a single flame burst into full-blown fire.

Two thumps sounded, then one more. Lils's hat and gloves hitting the floor, he reckoned. Glancing behind, he watched her try to unbutton her coat. With her fingers looking as brittle as blue porcelain, all they could do was tremble against the wet wool.

"Come over here to the fire, Lils."

He stretched his hand toward her. She stepped forward, grasped it, then settled down beside him.

"Land sakes, but aren't we a p-pair of i-icicles."

"Let me get those." Even though his fingers were not blue, they were numb, clumsy as an oaf's. The buttons felt like silver dollars that he was trying to push though dime-size holes.

This task would be impossible until his hands were warmer. He reached toward the flames at the same time Lils did. In unison, they shivered in their damp outerwear.

"Why are you letting me call you Lils?"

Damn! He hadn't intended to blurt that out. His plan had been to heat her up first, in front of the fireplace with a few kisses.

"I've decided to forgive you." She arched a dark auburn brow at him. "There is no reason we cannot be friends."

"Humph." With his fingers warmed, he reached

for her coat and slipped the buttons free. "I can think of one."

He slid the wet wool off her shoulders and tossed it somewhere. Removing his own coat, he pitched it in the same direction.

"And what would that be?" She knew what it was. The knowledge flared in her eyes along with the reflection of the snapping blaze.

He didn't speak, couldn't really. Not with his heart in his throat and his fingers moving toward the bodice of her dress.

The buttons parted so smoothly that he feared she would think he was accomplished at undressing ladies.

He had never been that man and now he knew why. There was only one woman for him. Not time, not distance, not even years of living a full and successful life had made him forget her.

He looked into her eyes and she held his gaze.

"You want to be my lover," Lils whispered, answering her own question.

He shook his head.

"No, Lils, I want to be your husband." He traced her jaw with one knuckle, then her throat. He rubbed the lace of her corset between his thumb and finger and felt the heat of her breast. "I'll be your lover, the father of your children. I'll be the man who never goes away."

"This is something for another time. I can't think about this now...not until my sister is safe."

"You're wrong, Lils. This is our time. We can't do a damn thing to help her in this storm—but Hanispree can't hurt her, either."

Trace leaned forward and kissed Lilleth. "This is our time."

She nodded, then kissed him back. "We shouldn't waste it."

She unbuttoned his shirt, then pushed it off his arms, trailing her fingers slowly over his skin, pausing at the muscle of his forearm and the bone at his wrist.

Baring her chest to the lapping heat of the flames, he traced the shape of her, from the full outer curves of her breasts, to the inner swell, then up her throat, where her pulse shimmied in her neck.

She touched the jagged L shape of his scar with the tip of her finger, silent for a long moment.

He squeezed her hand, but she winced.

"From the fall?" He kissed her palm, then lay it gently over his heart. "Will you marry me, Lils?"

"I told you a long time ago." Tears glittered in the corners of her eyes. "I will marry you and only you."

"Tonight. As soon as the snow quits." It had to be now. "Before something happens and someone snatches you away from me again."

"No one will ever do that, Trace. I'm older now. I would fight for you." She nodded, as though settling something in her mind. "I will marry you just as soon as my sister can stand up for me."

Lilleth leaned forward and pressed her breasts to his chest. A pair of hot circles branded his heart just as the scar had done over the years. But the scar had been cold, a reminder of loss.

Lils, crushing her body to the old wound, singed him with another brand. This one erased the past. Oddly, his elation at this moment was greater for having lived the loss.

Only one thing stood between him and his fantasy come to life.

A few pieces of clammy clothing.

In four swings of the pendulum on the mantel he had tossed away his trousers, long johns and socks.

Lilleth made even quicker work of her skirt, numerous underthings and boots.

She knelt across from him, looking like a mythical nymph…a goddess, bare and glorious. Her gaze took him in from shoulder to knee. It ignited a blaze across his flesh and kindled it deep in muscle and bone.

"I always figured you'd grow to be a beautiful woman, Lils, but you are so much more." He watched the fire warm her skin while he memorized each curve and hollow. "You make it hard for a man to breathe."

"And you make it impossible for a woman to have a respectable thought."

He caressed her bare shoulders, then pressed her back until she lay against the hearth rug.

Heat shimmered in her eyes. It sparked in her hair where it tumbled on the rug, wild and enticing. She made him feel feral in a way that he never had, as if he were a beast about to claim his mate.

He straddled her hips, his weight settling hot against her belly. Firelight licked her skin. It flushed her cheeks, her throat and the swell of her chest. It fondled her everyplace that he was about to.

He wanted to jump upon her all at once, to devour her, but this was a moment to be savored.

First, he tasted the curve of her waist.... He stroked the flare of her hip with his tongue and smoothed the fine goose bumps that had risen under his mouth with his hand.

An hour ago the storm had seemed a curse that fought and delayed them, but not any longer. Howling wind and whiteout snow would insure that every soul in Riverwalk stayed indoors. It gave them a precious bit of time before life returned, with a sister to be rescued and villains crushed.

For now, the only reality was his mouth showing her why grown men cried when she sang a love song.

The storm battered the front window, shook it until it nearly broke. At the same time it rattled the front door on its hinges.

With one touch, Trace did the same to her. His fingers moved over her skin, caressing, nuzzling, then settling down to explore that tender spot that had never been explored.

"I've always loved you," she whispered, rising to meet his mouth on her throat. "Even when I didn't want to."

"Good to know." He lifted up to smile down at her, and gently pinched her bottom. "I hope you always love me even when you don't want to."

He turned his attention to the swell of her chest, nibbling and pebbling her flesh with his tongue and teeth. She felt wicked and wonderful all at once. As though she had made herself into a delectable meal and allowed him to feast upon her.

"Trace?"

"Umm?" he answered, sounding husky.

"There's something I used to imagine when you were sitting at your desk." Her breathing came quicker now because his mouth was nibbling a lazy trail down her belly.

"Umm?" He paused.

"It's wicked. You'll be scandalized."

"Nothing between us will ever be wicked."

That couldn't be true when just the musky scent of his skin drove her to envision things that made her tremble.

"Sometimes, when you sit at your desk, I imagine that I am your book. You open me up, then—"

Just like that, before she could finish speaking, he stood up, his muscular thighs bunching and stretching while he lifted her.

With a sweep of his arm, he cleared the desk. Pens and ink bottles plinked on the floor.

He set her bare bottom on the polished wood and spread her thighs with big, firm hands.

"You're right, Lils. This might be a little bit wicked."

He touched his erection to her curls, then pressed the tip past her nether lips. Inch by slow inch he thrust into her. Squeeze by slow squeeze, she enfolded him.

His breathing sounded ragged.

"I love you, Lils," he said, leaning in close to her lips, but not quite kissing them. "Never anyone but you."

Cupping one hand under her buttocks, he climbed upon the table and slid her over the smooth surface without losing the precious contact of their joined bodies. He pressed her flat against the desk.

He drove into her and she met him. She owned him…or did he own her? She couldn't think, or breathe, or speak. With each thrust of his hips he made old heartaches disappear. The future dawned in an explosion of fireworks that shimmered in red and gold behind her eyelids.

"You weren't the only one who fantasized about

what could happen on this desk," Trace panted, while she felt the library fall slowly back into place.

"I wouldn't have guessed that a common book could lead to what we did." She trailed her fingers through his damp hair and rejoiced in the huff of his moist breath against her neck.

"Not any common book, Lils. You are my love story."

"You are a pea-brain, Perryman!" Alden shouted into the wind blowing stinging ice at his face. "You've gotten us lost in a blizzard."

"Never claimed to be a scout." Perryman looked down his razorlike nose and blinked his obsidian eyes. "Hotel's probably a little farther on."

"It had better be," Alden grumbled. "I paid you good money to get me those children and all you've got is us lost in a storm. You are a bungler."

He no longer cared if he hurt the fool's feelings or not. The man was an idiot. An apology later on and they would be friends again. It didn't even have to be sincere. Perryman was a dog in many ways, an insect-munching canine who welcomed the slightest show of approval from his master.

That was a pleasing thought. Alden Hanispree… the Master. And very soon he would be wealthy to go with it. Wealth would give him power; power would draw people to fawn over him. They'd be drooling all over themselves just to do what he wanted, no matter what it was.

All he needed was the brats. Now that he'd found them it would be a simple matter to get them back. Give that sister of Bethany's over to Perryman and he would no longer have to worry about her interfering.

Maybe he'd send Bethany a little gift from Perryman, just to let her know the easy times were over.

"Look!" Perryman shouted, only inches from Alden's ear. "There's a building ahead."

"You colossal moron!" He would have slapped Perryman's face with his glove, but the cold blow would have stung his own hand. "That's my insane asylum. You know I can't go there."

"You're the moron if you'd rather stay out here and freeze to death."

"Take me back to town."

"See those chimneys with the smoke coming out? I'm going there to get warm."

"You're going to get possessed, is what. You know those fires are kindled by ghosts."

"Warm is warm, my mother always said."

"Your mother left you while you were still at her teat."

Perryman shrugged. "Someone's mother had to say it, because it only makes sense."

"Come back here!" he shouted, but the fool turned his back and walked away.

"Stay here and die or face the ghouls," Perryman called over his shoulder.

"You'll pay for this!"

And he would, dearly. But for now Alden had no choice but to follow.

Lilleth stared down at six foot two inches of naked male sprawled midway down the staircase. Half an hour earlier he had been fondling her and she had been teasing him while they descended from the bedroom to the kitchen to get a bite of supper. Suddenly, desire had taken them over, completely and utterly. His kisses and her response had been too powerful to resist, and a deeper hunger than mere food had tumbled them down upon the middle step.

She knelt beside him now, sorry to say goodbye to this cozy nest, but it was time.

Touching his shoulder, she trailed her fingers to his jaw then tapped his nose.

"Wake up, Trace. It's raining."

"Not asleep," he groaned, and tried to pull her down to him. "In a pleasure daze."

"You're bound to be bruised on your backside," she mumbled into the sweat-dampened hair behind his ear. "It was kind of you to take the bottom position."

He popped one eye open, then arched that brow.

"Gallant," he agreed. He patted his belly. "Climb back on and I'll play the hero again. It's a small price to pay for seeing you riding me like a goddess taming her wild steed."

A flush heated her skin. After everything they had done over the past two and a half days, she was amazed that she had any modesty left.

Her blush was not the only thing rising, though. Trace tried to set her on top of him, but she scooted across the stair with more regret than she let on.

With the weather taking an unusual turn, rain of all things, it was time to find Bethany. The road to Hanispree would be passable even if the wooded trail would not be.

"Come on, we've got to hurry." She rushed down the steps to the lower floor, glancing quickly about the library. "Where did we leave our clothes?"

Trace stood up slowly, his muscles flexing while he stretched and groaned. She glanced away, but heard the wood stairs creaking with his weight while he came down.

If he touched her she was done. It might be hours before they made it to Hanispree.

She grabbed her coat off the rack and wrapped it around herself. Out of sight, out of mind.

The wool scratched her breasts and tickled her belly. Before Trace, she'd never paid much attention to what touched her skin. Now all she wanted on it were his hands…and his mouth. What a wicked creature she had become.

"Lils," Trace whispered, coming up from behind. He reached around, pulled the coat open, then slipped his hands between the wool and her belly. "If you want to get to the hospital you'd better at least put on your underclothes."

"You're a fine one to give orders, Mr. Naked Ballentine."

He turned her around and nibbled a trail between her ear and her throat.

"Oh," she moaned, and leaned into his lips. Her intended was dangerous. With his mouth alone he could turn her into a spineless creature who cared for nothing more than coupling with him.

Somehow during these precious days, lying under, beside or on top of Trace, she had come to understand her mother…and to forgive her. They were the same, except that poor Mama had never been able to distinguish a good man from a dissolute one.

Lilleth gathered her wits— or what she had left of them—and pushed away from her trustworthy man, because trustworthy or not, he was temptation incarnate.

"Get dressed." She tapped her toe and Trace sighed. He shoved his fingers through his matted hair.

"Who knows what might be happening at the mental hospital while you and I dally away precious time?" she asked.

"Dally, Lils?" He strode to the fireplace, where trousers tangled with bloomers and coarse red long johns lay beneath a delicate ivory camisole. "Love doesn't dally, it binds. The minute we free Bethany, we're headed for the preacher."

"And I'll lead the parade," she said, crossing her arms over her chest. "Now put on some clothes."

Traveling the main road to the hospital held some risk, but as far as Trace could determine there was no other way to get there. The woodland path was impassable with the snow piled in drifts and broken tree limbs littering the way.

Not only was he concerned about encountering Alden and Perryman, but the weather had taken an odd turn. Rain had switched back into snow almost the moment they'd stepped out of the lending library.

They were still a quarter mile away from the hospital when lightning exploded with a long, muffled crackle. It sounded far-off, but wouldn't be.

An eerie loop of light illuminated the sky. It looked like a static halo. He'd never seen the likes of this but he'd read about it. Thunder snow happened when bitter cold clashed with warm air in some odd and unusual way. Mostly, it happened in the spring, but also in the fall once in a great while.

"That was spooky," Lils whispered, huddling closer to his side.

"Can you still run?"

She nodded. Red curls pulled away from his coat, full of static. She dashed out ahead of him, then turned back to wink. Lilleth put on a brave face, but she had to be frightened.

Hell, he was nearly shaking in his socks, watching her run up the wide road ahead of him. Bolts of electricity hit the ground all around. It etched spiny fingers through bare trees and gave the snow a freakish white glow.

Lils was still a runner, faster than he was by far. She paused at the front gate to wait for him.

When he got there she rose on her toes to kiss him. Then, as they had plotted on the way, she headed round the back, toward Mrs. Murphy's room, to make sure all was well with the children, while Trace—in character as Clark—entered through the lobby to find out what he could.

He was greeted by a merrily snapping fire in the big hearth and the rotund Nurse Fry gesturing wildly to Nurse Goodhew.

The drama between them was intense. They either failed to notice him come in, or downright ignored him.

"I heard it myself," Nurse Fry wailed. "A baby crying, and no doubt about it."

"We have no infants here, Nurse. Pull yourself together."

"No human infants." Nurse Fry wrung her hands. "I won't be going back in those dark halls again, I can tell you."

"If you value your job you will."

"I will not! Not alone, at any rate. It's not just the baby crying anymore. There's a boy, a frightening apparition that pops out from anywhere." Nurse Fry covered her mouth and shook her head. "Not an hour ago it tugged on my apron strings."

"Really, Miss Fry, have you been getting into the drug cabinet?" Nurse Goodhew stared down her long nose at her employee.

Lightning shocked the lobby, making the women appear rather spooky themselves. If Trace didn't know who the ghost child was, he might be frightened, as well.

If one were to imagine ghosts and goblins gliding in and out of walls, this would be the night for it.

"Good evening, ladies," Trace declared.

"Mr. Clarkly." Nurse Goodhew shot him a frown. "Why must you always come when the weather is foul? Do you enjoy dripping all over my floors?"

As a matter of fact, he did. That particular trick had come in useful on a few occasions.

"Why, no. That is, I don't mean to. It's just that the weather is normally foul. It is November, after all." He shook his coat to make sure that the snow splattered on the floor. "I've brought books. Since you and Nurse Fry seem to be engaged, I'll hand them out myself. Won't be but a few moments."

He took several steps toward the hallway where the well-appointed patient rooms were.

"Stop right there!" demanded Nurse Goodhew. "Not one more step."

He continued on for five more. "It's no trouble at all." He meant to get into those rooms. He suspected that's where Bethany had been taken.

When the weather cleared and Hanispree ventured from the hotel, he wouldn't have the courage to confront her in her old cell. That had to be the reason she had been moved.

Nurse Goodhew abandoned her argument with Nurse Fry and ran toward the hallway, cutting Trace off.

"Give me those books and go home, Mr. Clarkly."

"I believe Nurse Fry looks ill. Perhaps if we take her down this corridor and open each of the doors, between the two of us we can convince her that there is no such thing as the wandering dead."

"She will simply have to accept my word on that."

He resolved to get into those rooms even if he had to tie the unpleasant Goodhew to a chair. Lilleth counted on him to free her sister. He would get Bethany out of this hell pit today, before Hanispree got here.

"What if Nurse Fry is correct? Shouldn't we assure ourselves that she is not?"

"Don't blather, Mr. Clarkly. There is no boy and there is no baby. It's bad enough having Mr. Hanis—"

"Mr. Hanispree is in attendance?" Trace's stomach pitched.

He could not have gotten here in the storm. That meant he had come before that and been here three days, and possibly Perryman with him.

No matter what it took, this would end today.

"Perhaps he'd care for a book, if you will point me to his room?" he asked mildly, in spite of the turmoil in his gut.

"Mr. Hanispree is indisposed."

"Terrified of the ghosts is what he is." Mrs. Fry pointed a plump finger at Trace. "He knows the truth."

Mrs. Goodhew heaved a long-suffering sigh. "You are dismissed, Nurse Fry. Take your belongings and don't come back."

A spear of lightning brightened the room at the same time that Nurse Fry opened the door.

An older couple blew inside with the wind. The nurse hurried past them, sailing out into the night.

Trace blinked, Clark style, more than surprised to see the couple about in the storm.

"I'm Mr. Horace Bolt. I've come to commit my wife," the man said, his voice harsh as sand. "She's losing her mind."

"I'm saner than you, you old goat!" Mrs. Bolt said. She gazed at Trace, clearly noticing his alphabetized stack of books.

"I'd like to speak with Mr. Hanispree himself," Mr. Bolt demanded.

"He is not available," Nurse Goodhew answered with a sniff. "I'm certain I can help you."

"I'm rich. I'll pay a lot." Mr. Bolt withdrew a wad of bills from his money pouch. "Go get him."

"You won't lock me up." Mrs. Bolt continued to stare at Trace. "I'll pay Hanispree even more to set me free."

At the sight of the cash, Nurse Goodhew's demeanor softened. "We are not concerned with money here at Hanispree. The well-being of our patients is of paramount importance to us," she said, acting her part so well she might have been a Ballentine. "Perhaps Mr. Hanispree will see you tomorrow."

"He will see me right this minute or the deal is off." Mr. Bolt stuffed the cash into his coat pocket. "Give my wife a room before she drives us all to distraction."

"And who," Mrs. Bolt demanded, pointing her finger at Clark, "is this? You ought to be more careful about who you expose that wad of money to, Mr. Bolt."

"Clarkly," Trace answered. "Mr. Clark Clarkly."

"That ridiculous librarian?" She stepped up close to him, her eyes narrowed in her round, pink-cheeked face. "I heard he'd retired."

"Without a word of warning," Mr. Bolt added. "Just up and quit."

Trace nodded at his mother, then his father. "Sometimes a career won't let you go even when you try to give it up."

"Who would want to be a dreary librarian, anyway?" Mrs. Bolt observed.

"Dreary or not, Mrs. Bolt," her husband replied, "it's a job and someone's got to do it."

"If you think so, ma'am...sir—" he wanted to hug them, but his shoelace made him lose his balance, and he slipped to one knee "—I reckon I'll give the job another go."

Mr. and Mrs. Bolt, the wealthy and overbearing couple, turned as one to face Nurse Goodhew.

"If you value your job, miss, you'll send Mr. Hanispree to the lobby." Mr. Bolt demanded. "If not I'll fetch him myself."

"Get him this very moment!" Trace's mother snapped her fingers at the nurse, then turned and winked. "I find that I can't endure my overbearing husband for another instant. Please show me all your very best rooms."

Chapter Fifteen

Lilleth hustled around the corner toward the back door. Jess was supposed to have made sure that it remained unlocked. He would have been expecting her to return well before now, though.

She was more than a little nervous to know how the children had fared with Mrs. Murphy. She was an old lady and two young ones would be a challenge. Jess was capable, but because of the storm, it had been three days.

Thankfully, the knob turned in her hand. Before she went inside she went to the woodpile and picked up three logs. There was not any smoke coming from the chimneys of the inmates' quarters, so they must have run out.

She stacked the wood beside the door, then returned to get more. On her next trip she tried to carry four logs, but ended up dropping one. She bent to pick it up.

A hand clamped down on her shoulder. It spun her about so that she lost her balance and fell over.

She looked up into the obsidian eyes of the bug eater. He hovered over her as though she were a roach and he was about to chomp on her with those unnaturally sharp teeth.

"You idiot!" she swore.

"Look who's on the ground and who's standing up. Who's the idiot now, pretty lady?"

She was, of course. She hadn't been talking to him at all. To let a man creep up on her unaware was the height of folly.

"You've got me now, I reckon." Reaching for a log to defend herself with would be a mistake. Perryman would disarm her easily. Her only defense would be surprise, so she sighed and gave a helpless shrug. "Whatever will you do with me?"

"That's for me to know. It ain't wise to tell a woman too much."

"You're right, of course." She reached a hand for him to help her off the ground. "It's just that if you tell me where we're going I can walk there instead of you having to drag me."

"Could be I want to drag you." He ignored her hand.

"Could be you'll be sorry for it," she snapped, even if it meant revealing that she was not as helpless as she pretended.

Perryman rubbed the back of his head. Good, it looked as if the two blows she had dealt him with the shovel still smarted.

"Walk, then, but I'm right behind you...breathing down your neck."

"You might want to tell me where I'm walking to."

"You'll see when we get there. Just march your helpless self right through them trees."

Across a frozen meadow and then through a copse of icy-branched trees appeared a gardener's shed made of stone.

Perryman opened the door, gripping her wrist with fingers that felt more like cold bones than flesh and blood. He shoved her inside and shut the door behind them.

Cold air crept up her legs. It nipped and swirled about her. The interior of the shed was too dark to see anything. Metal scraped metal, probably a bolt being shot home.

Perryman was about five feet away from her, judging by the rasp of his breathing. A match hissed, then a lantern flared to life.

"You poor man, is this where Alden makes you sleep?" she asked, spotting a crude pile of blankets that made for a tattered bed in the corner. A shovel and a pick leaned against the wall beside it.

Perryman must have noticed her looking at them.

"I'm no fool, lady." He snatched the tools and

tossed them out the door. To her relief, she didn't hear the lock slide back into place. "I won't forget what happened the last time you had your hands around a shovel. Just since you asked, I sleep in the big house, all warm and cozy. The gardener's shed is for you, for as long as I want to keep you here. The pick and shovel are for when I don't."

The hiss of his bare palms scratching against each other filled the room. He chuckled, obviously expecting her to cringe.

Well, she wasn't ready to cringe, not just yet.

"I hit you because you were a stranger." She walked up close to him, pretending that she was not his victim. "A mother has a duty to protect her little girls."

"S'at so?" He pinched her chin between his stringy fingers. "I know you ain't a mama. Those kids you got hiding in the crazy house belong to Hanispree."

"If you believe that, why are you here and not turning them over to your employer?" She wrenched her chin from his hold and walked to a far corner of the shed. Perryman followed her, his grim shadow crossing the dirt floor.

Thunder shook the building. The lightning must have struck only feet away for it to make stone tremble. For an instant, it rattled Perryman and distracted him.

Lilleth's foot kicked something solid that had been covered in dirt and straw.

"Got me a plan. Guess it don't matter to tell you, though, since you won't be saying anything to anybody anymore." He grinned. In the dim lamplight his sharp teeth glittered with a feral snarl. "I'm not giving those kids to Alden, not for the pitiful price he was going to pay. My pockets won't be big enough for all the cash he'll have to hand over. A man ought to get a fair price for something another man wants so bad."

"You're smart as well as handsome, Mr. Perryman." She sat down on the floor, then fluffed out her skirt. Just under her derriere pressed the cold hard shape of a spike.

"I'm not a fool who can be charmed, so don't you try." He snatched a rope from a hook on the wall. "Take off your coat."

She had no choice; she did it. He tied her hands behind her back and tested the knot with a vicious tug.

Lilleth doubted that her mother's suitors had prepared her for this battle. Not a single one of them had ever gotten close enough to disable her with a rope.

"You are no fool, Mr. Perryman, and I am no charmer."

But her voice was. She settled onto the floor with a sigh, feeling the cold shape of the ten-inch weapon beneath her. She hoped it was sharp.

She smiled up at her captor's black scowl and began to sing.

* * *

Trace watched Alden Hanispree stride into the lobby.

The short, cowardly man glanced fearfully at the door that led to the inmates' quarters, then over his shoulder.

He spotted the money that Trace's father held, and seemed to forget about what might be following him. His hands twitched and his avaricious grin flickered in the stabs of lightning flashing through the windows.

"My word, Mr. Hanispree. Are you well?" Trace's mother asked. "You look as though you've seen a ghost."

Clearly, his parents had been doing some investigation. They knew exactly where to place a dig.

"Or they've seen you," Clark added, peering hard at the man through his spectacles. "Unpleasant business any way you look at it."

Hanispree hadn't appeared pale before his mother fired her jab, but he did now.

"See here." His father waved the cash at Alden. "That's enough rubbish talk. I've come to do business. I want the best room you have for Mrs. Bolt."

"It had better be," Trace's mother declared, then turned her back on the transaction.

She walked across the room to stand beside Trace, who appeared to be warming himself near the big snapping fire in the hearth. In reality, he was studying the situation in the room, figuring how he could use it to get to Bethany.

"What are you doing here, Mrs. Bolt?" he whispered.

"A lucky thing for you, my dear, that your brother is nosy. Cooper smelled trouble, what with that odd Perryman fellow spying on your young lady. Quite naturally, we began an investigation. Alden Hanispree is a greedy twit, I do have to say…separating children from their mother. I hope we are in time to help sort this mess out."

"Look here, Hanispree," Trace's father exclaimed. "I'm not handing over this money until I've seen every room you have."

"Where is Miss Preston?" His mother jabbed Trace in the ribs with her elbow. From across the room, he thought Nurse Goodhew noticed.

He handed his mother a book and opened it.

"Here we have an otter," he said loudly. "Cavorting with its two little babies. Otters are devoted creatures, did you know?"

"I'd like to see one for myself one day, young man."

"They live in dark places," he said, not knowing if that was true or not. "With lots of other otters living in dark places."

He inclined his head toward the door behind Nurse Goodhew's desk.

"Oh, I see." His mother tapped her finger on the

page. "I believe I'll take a trip to the zoo, Mr. Clarkly. I'd love to see a pair as sweet as these two."

"Nurse Goodhew!" she called, when it looked as though the nurse would sink down into the chair at her desk. "If my husband finds a suitable room to lock me up in, I will be bringing a boxcar full of belongings. I'll not even leave him a pair of my bloomers."

She glared at Mr. Bolt, then focused her attention back on the nurse. "Please show me where my goods will be stored. Naturally, I will require access to them day and night."

"We have plenty of room for whatever you bring."

As far as Goodhew would be concerned, the more of Mrs. Bolt's worldly goods she brought with her the better. As part of his investigation Trace had discovered that the nurse sold the patients' personal belongings to add a tidy amount to her already high wages.

"We don't think of our guests as being shut away, Mrs. Bolt. We treat them as we would our own dear families. Hanispree is a resort more than anything else." Goodhew pointed to the door behind her. "There ought to be room for all your things back in storage."

It took all his self-control not to snort at the lie. Behind that door were things far more precious than belongings to be stored.

"I'll have a look. Since my husband is dumping me here, I might as well see to it."

"We'll think of all that tomorrow, after we've seen to your comfort. Let me find you a lovely room down the hall, then your husband can be on his way."

"You'll rue the day you did this to me, Mr. Bolt."

"Mr. Hanispree, my wife is not herself these days. She's a bit addled, if you know what I mean." His father touched his temple, then slipped the money back into his pocket. "I'll see to the room now. Kindly lead the way."

Hanispree gave Bolt what ought to have been a cordial smile, but on his corrupt face it was a mask.

"As it happens we have a few lovely rooms available just down this hall."

"Mr. Hanispree!" Nurse Goodhew hustled out from behind the desk. "Now would not be the time to show our best rooms. Some of the patients are receiving treatments."

There were no patients in there, only a captive. Time was up; Trace needed to get to Bethany before the doctor gave her a "treatment" that she would never recover from.

"I'll come along." Trace walked up to his father and stood shoulder to shoulder with him. "The treatments will certainly go easier with a book to read. I'm sure that Mr. Bolt would appreciate seeing an example of the care his wife will receive at your hands."

Nurse Goodhew shot him a look. She clearly didn't trust him. "I'll be back shortly," she said, giving his mother a nod. "I'm going to find you a nice big storage room."

Trace's mother frowned. The otters were in danger was what she would be thinking.

"Not a single one of these rooms is up to standard, Mr. Hanispree. My wife is used to being pampered in every detail. You do have servants? I haven't seen any."

Hanispree had not hesitated to open each door on the ground floor, and most of them on the second.

Wherever they had put Bethany, it wasn't here.

"I've a capital idea!" Trace exclaimed. "Mr. Bolt, why don't you have the attic remodeled for your wife?"

"Couldn't hurt to see the place, might have some nice views. Are there windows up there, Mr. Hanispree?"

"Not a single one. The attic won't do for your wife at all."

Because that's where Bethany was.

"Nonsense." His father clamped his fist over Hanispree's arm. "I insist on seeing it. Lead the way."

Trace didn't wait to be led anywhere. He dropped the books and dashed toward the back stairs at the end of the hall.

Nurse Goodhew's voice brought him up short.

"Mr. Hanispree!" she shouted from the landing

of the stairs. "I found this heathen child in the storage area. I believe he belongs to you?"

"Indeed he does." Alden Hanispree strode forward and took the struggling, gagged boy from Goodhew. "What about the other one?"

"I'll fetch her right away." Goodhew snorted. "I believe we've found our ghosts, Mr. Hanispree."

"Why is the boy gagged?" Trace asked.

"He is a detestable child with much too much to say." She rubbed her backside as she retreated down the hall.

"Mr. Bolt." Hanispree squeezed Jess's shoulder, making him wince. "If you wouldn't mind coming back tomorrow?"

Trace leaped from the second step of the attic stairway, on the run. He shoved Hanispree to the floor and caught Jess to him. The gag was tight. The more Trace worked at the knot, the harder it held.

A moan drifted down the hallway, sliding along the walls and creeping across the floor.

An apparition appeared bit by bit. She came into view slowly, appearing at the top of the stairs. First her head, then her shoulders, and at last the rest of her ghoulish self.

Trace continued to work at the wet bindings, but couldn't avert his gaze from his sister's performance.

She drifted toward Hanispree, where he lay sprawled on the floor. She hunched her shoulders and stretched out her arms, reaching for him.

"Killer…" she wailed. "Murderer…"

"Keep her away from me," he squealed.

"Her who?" Trace's father asked, reaching down a hand. "Your nurse has already gone downstairs."

Hanispree began to sputter words that made no sense. He wagged his finger at Hannah. "The woman who looks like she drowned," he finally yelped in a trembling voice.

Trace and his father glanced about. They shrugged their shoulders.

"Show me the attic, man. There's no one here but me and the librarian…and this boy who has been treated so miserably."

Clearly, Jess had something to say, but with the gag in his mouth his words were stifled. Trace worked harder at the knot while Jess tried to pull the cloth away.

"Hold still, Jess. It's beginning to loosen."

The boy stood as still as he could, but Trace felt the tension strung tight inside him.

Hannah "levitated" forward, moaning. She drew a web of moss across Hanispree's face. He scurried backward, looking like a crab trying to escape a seagull.

"You killed me!" she moaned.

"I never killed anybody, I swear it!"

"You drowned me in the pond…oooh."

Actually, the pond was frozen, and Alden wouldn't have been able to do that if he had tried.

Luckily, the man was too panicked to notice Hannah's mistake.

"I suppose a murderer might be haunted, don't you agree, Mr. Bolt?"

"It would be hard to avoid that."

Jess stamped his foot.

Hanispree clawed at his collar. "I didn't kill you. You're…"

All of a sudden he lunged to his feet and ran for the attic stairs.

They all followed. Hanispree stopped at one of several doors in the dim attic and fished a key ring out of his pocket, his fingers skittering over the choices. He selected one, then opened the door, banging it hard against the wall.

"There you are!" he shouted. "Sound and hale! I never killed anyone."

Not yet, at any rate. In the center of the room was a chair with straps—a spinner. It was a device that was supposed to spin patients until the blood left their head, and with it their mental illness.

It whirled and clicked as it turned. This was a torture that could go on for hours in the name of treatment.

Jess ran to his mother and hugged her about the waist.

The person in the spinning chair was Dr. Merlot, his face green, and vomit stinking up the front of his jacket.

Served the fellow right for messing with one of the Preston women.

Trace would have laughed had it not been for the fact that Jess's panic didn't subside with finding his mother.

Bethany, apparently more adept at knots than he was, yanked the gag from her son's head in under ten seconds.

"Perryman took Auntie Lilleth!" he shouted.

Bethany folded her boy in her arms and rocked him, wept over him. "Where, Jess?"

"I don't know. That nurse grabbed me before I could find out."

Jess turned to his uncle, but didn't leave the safety of his mother's arms. "Since it wasn't Ma that you killed, you must have let Perryman kill Auntie Lils. There's still the spare ghost."

Trace's sister shook her weeds at Hanispree and screeched.

The man shook his head. Drool pooled in the corners of his mouth and, by heaven, he had peed his pants.

Trace was at Alden's throat, squeezing, threatening, and wishing he could kill the man. "Where the hell is Lilleth?"

Hannah drifted forward. She draped her funeral gauze over Alden's pasty face.

"Gardener's shed…in the woods," he croaked.

Trace didn't feel the stairs beneath his shoes, nor

his lungs aching or his heart beating, but he did notice the inmates gathered in front of the fireplace in the lobby.

He took in the details of the scene as he dashed out the front door.

A dozen people in tattered clothing turning their cold bodies in circles, warming to the flames. Mrs. Murphy blew him a kiss.

His mother smiled and cooed to Mary. Nurse Goodhew cursed out loud, because she had been tied to the chair behind her desk.

The door to the prison rooms stood wide-open.

It seemed that her only weapon would be the stake, if she could even grasp it with her hands tied behind her back.

The very thought of using that metal shaft made her shiver. Last time she had defended herself with something pointed, Trace had nearly lost his life.

If she thought that Trace wouldn't find her, she would use it with barely a breath of hesitation.

But he would find her eventually, once he realized she was missing. The man did follow clues for a living.

She would have to escape on her own—and soon. How could she ever draw another breath if the same thing happened again? History had been known to repeat itself.

Suddenly the sharpened metal underneath her felt as a much a threat as a help.

"You look scared, lady."

"What?" Perryman hadn't spoken in some time, and in her worry over the spike she hadn't noticed that he was staring at her as if she were his dinner. "Well, yes I am. Trembling, in fact."

"I have to punish you." He stood up, awkward limbed, looking like a gaunt scarecrow rising from a pumpkin patch.

"Not if you don't want to."

Oh, dear. The flash of his grin, malicious in the lamplight, told her that he did want to. That he would enjoy it.

"You did bean me with the shovel. It hurt right smart. You insulted me."

"Surely you can understand a mother wanting to protect her children."

"Surely can't. My mother was a slut. Turned me away before I knew how to call her one. Besides, you ain't nobody's mother."

"My mother was a slut, too." Maybe common ground would soothe him. "But I loved her just the same."

"Then you were a fool." He clapped his hands. "Let's eat."

Incredibly, in spite of the cold, Perryman began to undress. His flesh pebbled, but that didn't stop him from removing every stitch.

His naked body and Trace's resembled each other in the same way that a sway-backed nag resembled a wild stallion.

Ribs and hip bones jutting out from his gaunt flesh made him appear a ghoulish creature who might have escaped from the pages of one of Trace's horror books.

While he struggled with the knot on a small black bag, Lilleth thought frantically. How would she outwit him?

"There you are, you pretty little beast," Perryman murmured, drawing something dark and squirming out of the bag.

"Eat it." He squatted before her. "Chew it slow… and smile when you swallow it."

No! No matter what, she would not eat the inch-long stinkbug struggling between Perryman's grimy fingernails.

He pinched it and smeared its guts against her lips. She wanted to gag, to scream, but that would mean opening her mouth. Panic threatened the edges of her control. She shivered with the effort of containing it.

She would not be forced to this vileness, to be a victim of his depravity. If she ate the insect, what would come next? She suspected this was only the first of many wicked things that he planned to force upon her.

Her lips felt slick with the bug ooze that he'd

smeared there. She turned her head, wiped her mouth on her shoulder. She spit.

"That wasn't polite." He dug in the bag again. "Maybe something more moist? More squirmy? I don't like to eat alone. That would offend me."

He stared at her chest, tilting his head this way and that. He licked his lips.

Placing a hand between her breasts, he pushed her down to the dirt.

She struggled, but it was all for show. If she were going to use her weapon, she would need to be lying flat to reach it. If she lay down of her own accord, he would become suspicious.

So she cowered in the dirt, giving a show of fear and submission. And the truth was, she had never been this frightened of a man.

Bent at an awkward angle, her arms hurt. She breathed deeply and steadily in an attempt to ignore the pain.

She gripped the spike, watching for her moment and praying that it would be soon.

History could not repeat. Trace was not here. He couldn't be injured.

Perryman came down upon her slowly, his chest and his hips pressing her against the dirt. He touched her lips with what could only be a giant maggot. It squirmed and so did he.

It was this moment or not at all.

Lilleth clutched the cold metal in her tied fists.

Her elbows felt as if they would pop at the joints. She wanted to vomit.

The memory of the sound of Trace's flesh tearing, the scent of his blood and the stickiness of it on her hands, made her scream. She didn't want to. It weakened her.

She bit Perryman's ear. He screeched and jerked up far enough for her to turn and lift the blade

To her complete horror, she spotted Trace standing in the doorway of the shed, his face consumed with anger, his teeth clenched in rage.

He lunged. The tip of the spike was pointed at his chest.

Lilleth tried to move it out of the way, but Perryman's weight held her. Just as before, she could do nothing to prevent the disaster unfolding.

This time Trace would die. She would kill him by her own hand.

Lilleth shrieked. The howl filled her head. She heard the crunching of bone. The scent of blood filled her nose.

She managed to lift her knees. She ground them into Perryman's belly, shoving his weight away from her.

Arms grabbed her, held her tight. Someone picked her up off the ground to take her who knew where. Frenzied, she kicked out, gnashing her teeth, seeking his throat.

"Lils." The arms around her began to rock. A

large, firm hand stroked her hair. It cradled her head to a stallion's chest. "It's all right, Lils, I've got you."

Jess rushed forward. He wrapped his arms about her and Trace.

"It's all right, Auntie," he said, out of breath. "You're safe now. We all are, even Ma."

"Bethany?" Lilleth looked about through tear-flooded eyes and saw her sister, clutching her skirt high and rushing through the door of the shed. Trace made room for Bethany in the hug.

Other people gathered in the doorway. A middle-aged woman Lilleth did not know brushed a tear from her eye.

A man who looked like Trace, but a generation older, held Alden in front of him. Hanispree struggled, but the man had his arm locked around his neck.

"Kidnapping carries a hearty penalty," a young woman said. She strode in the door, swiping moss away from her face.

She walked up to Perryman, who was detained in the corner by a big, if thin, man Lilleth recognized as one of the inmates.

"Quit your blubbering, man," the young woman said. "It's only a broken nose."

"Cover that man up. He's perfectly revolting," the middle-aged woman said to Trace.

He kissed Lilleth, then went and plucked a filthy rag from the corner and dropped it on Perryman.

Lilleth hugged her sister's neck, and they both wept. Jess patted their shoulders.

After a moment she looked for Trace. He stood beside the moss-covered woman dressed in gauze, speaking quietly to her. The woman glanced at Lilleth and smiled, then clapped her hands.

When Trace came back to her, she lifted his coat, skimming her hands over his shirt, searching for blood. "I thought for sure I'd stabbed you."

"I thought so, too." He touched his shirt where the old scar was. "Saw the spike coming right at me."

"I couldn't turn it away. I tried.... I don't know how...."

"It was Pa that turned the stake away." Jess looked at his mother.

Bethany cupped his cheeks, then kissed his forehead. "I'm sure it was," she answered. "He watches over us from above."

"Not above, Ma. Right here. I saw him as clear as I'm seeing you. He pushed the point of the spike down. After that he went over to Uncle Alden and kicked him in the butt."

Alden Hanispree fainted. The man holding him let him drop, then anchored him with a boot to the chest.

"I understand, son," Bethany said. "It's been a frightening day. It's only natural that you might imagine your father's ghost was here. But in the light of day, there is no such thing."

"Mrs. Murphy wouldn't say so," Jess answered. "But Pa wasn't a ghost, he was more like an angel."

"I believe you, Jess." Lilleth spoke up for him.

She did believe it. Trace had been coming down on that spike. She was not the one who had moved it out of the way.

"So do I," Trace declared. "Never expected to say so, but the fact is, I'm not dead and I ought to be."

"There's more to the universe than we mortals can understand," the pretty older woman declared. She smiled and she, too, looked like Trace. "I understand there's to be a wedding."

Trace stood before the fireplace in the library, kissing his bride...at last. At long last.

The ceremony hadn't taken place the moment Bethany had been freed, because according to the women of the family, weddings involved more than just the bride and groom being willing.

To his dismay, they had swept Lilleth away an hour after the town marshal had come to escort the criminals to jail, and they had not let Trace near her since.

It had taken four very long days to arrange things to the ladies' satisfaction. Lace ribbons and satin sashes draped the library from ceiling to floor in what he had been assured was a romantic setting to thrill his bride.

As far as he was concerned, a romantic setting

would be Lilleth wearing nothing but blushing skin, soaking in the bath or reclining on the bed...or the stairs.

Since his mother, his sister, and Bethany, too, had their hearts set on all the frills and frippery, the only thing to do was grin through each prewedding task.

At last a feast was prepared and a guest invited. Mrs. Murphy had been confused at first. Wasn't Lilleth already Trace's spirit bride?

Happy events, Lilleth had explained to her, were often repeated in the great beyond, given that folks had eternity to celebrate. This pleased Mrs. Murphy no end.

Cooper had come for the wedding, but had been no help in rushing Trace to the altar. Very clearly, he had taken a shine to Bethany...and Bethany had taken, if not a fancy, at least an interest in him.

With Alden going to jail for a very long time, Bethany had become the new owner of the mental hospital. Seeing to the inmates' comfort and moving them all to the fancy wing of the facility had taken time away from hammering down the wedding details.

The longest delay had been due to the wedding gown. Trace's mother, Hannah and Bethany had fussed over the secret garment for all the four days.

In the end, with the waiting finished, he had to admit it was worth the delay.

His Lils glided toward him looking as if she were

wrapped in the mists of heaven. A lump lodged smack in his throat when she smiled at him.

They stood in front of his brother Jace to recite their vows. Jace was the only Ballentine to not take a position in the family business. His was a higher calling, as he liked to explain.

Finally, the promises were given. Lils was Trace's from this day forward. He was hers for now and forever more.

Cheers erupted in the library. Lilleth and Trace were now "the Ballentines." A couple, man and wife.

After a lifetime of wishing, he was finally kissing his bride. His mind itched with visions of things to come later.

A tap on his shoulder reminded him that this was not later.

"I'd like to welcome my daughter-in-law, son," his mother said.

She wrapped Lilleth in a great hug and whispered in her ear. When his mother transferred her to his father for a welcome, he whispered things, too. Things that made Lilleth grin and nod her head.

If he'd eavesdropped correctly, his father had just given Lilleth a job. Trace would have something to say about her being a spy. He didn't like it. One investigator in the family was treacherous enough.

Trace snatched his wife back from her brand-new father-in-law and tucked her close to his side. She was his, and that meant protecting her.

"There's a rule against working in the field when you become a mother," he whispered in her ear.

"Don't be silly, Trace." She wrapped her arms around his neck, looked him in the eye, then rose up on her toes to kiss him. "That's a weak rule, according to your sister."

"Rules are rules," he recited.

"And yet you broke the biggest one of all, and here you are, employed and forgiven."

"And given a raise," he grumbled.

"Life is going to be grand." She patted his cheek. "Not a dull moment."

"I'm thinking of keeping the library open, right here in Riverwalk." That sounded safe.

"You'd die of boredom and make me miserable in the process."

Lilleth wriggled out from under his arm and dashed across the room to embrace her sister.

That one action told him just what life would be like. He would try and hold Lils to him, to protect her as a man ought to, and she would dash away and do whatever she wanted.

Life with Lilleth Ballentine would not be a sweet and predictable fairy tale. He thanked God for that. It would be earthy, exciting and wonderful. She had been right when she told him he would be bored with the life of a librarian, even if it was in the name of safety.

Candlelight, satin swags and the aromas of the

feast did make for a night of romance. In spite of his impatience to get to this moment, Trace wouldn't have changed an instant of it.

The guests would leave soon. Then the night would belong to him and his bride.

The front door opened. Sarah blew inside on a dark cold wind, carrying the latest books she had borrowed. The little girl shivered in her thin coat. It was well past the time that she ought to be out.

Trace took a step toward her, then stopped when he spotted Jess doing the same. The look on the boy's face was one that he remembered on his own face many years ago.

Jess was smitten. He walked toward little Sarah in a Cupid-induced trance.

Sarah smiled at him. Jess grinned back and lifted the books from her arms.

That just went to show that love was timeless. As far as Mrs. Murphy was concerned it crossed eternity.

Trace caught Lilleth's gaze from where she stood across the room, speaking to her sister. He nodded his head toward Jess, who shifted from foot to foot, looking nervous and enraptured all at once.

Lilleth elbowed her sister in the ribs, then discreetly pointed toward the children.

Bethany covered her mouth with her hand to hide a chuckle. Lilleth whispered in her ear, and whatever she said made her sister's eyes widen in horror.

Lilleth laughed out loud, then looked at Trace, the love in her eyes as tangible as a kiss.

His bride touched her heart. She winked and blew him a kiss.

* * * * *

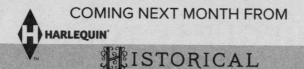

COMING NEXT MONTH FROM

HARLEQUIN®

HISTORICAL

Available November 19, 2013

THE TEXAS RANGER'S HEIRESS WIFE
by Kate Welsh
(Western)

Helena Conwell has built a successful ranch, but now raiders are hungry for her land. Only one man can protect her—Brendan Kane, the wild Texas Ranger she married at gunpoint.

NOT JUST A WALLFLOWER
A Season of Secrets • by Carole Mortimer
(Regency)

Ellie Rosewood is the talk of the *ton*. Her guardian, Justin, Duke of Royston, has one job—to find her a husband. But confirmed rake Justin wants Ellie all for himself!

RUNNING FROM SCANDAL
Bancrofts of Barton Park • by Amanda McCabe
(Regency)

David Marton lives a quiet life, until Emma Bancroft comes sweeping back into his world. She will never be the right woman for him, but sometimes temptation is too hard to resist....

FALLING FOR THE HIGHLAND ROGUE
The Gilvrys of Dunross
by Ann Lethbridge
(Regency)

Disgraced lady Charity West lives in the city's seedy underbelly. She's used and abused, yearning for freedom, and her distrust of men runs deep...until she meets Highland rogue Logan Gilvry.

YOU CAN FIND MORE INFORMATION ON UPCOMING HARLEQUIN® TITLES, FREE EXCERPTS AND MORE AT WWW.HARLEQUIN.COM.

HHCNM1113

REQUEST YOUR FREE BOOKS!

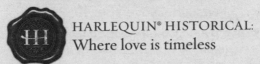

HARLEQUIN® HISTORICAL:
Where love is timeless

2 FREE NOVELS PLUS 2 FREE GIFTS!

YES! Please send me 2 FREE Harlequin® Historical novels and my 2 FREE gifts (gifts are worth about $10). After receiving them, if I don't wish to receive any more books, I can return the shipping statement marked "cancel." If I don't cancel, I will receive 6 brand-new novels every month and be billed just $5.44 per book in the U.S. or $5.74 per book in Canada. That's a savings of at least 16% off the cover price! It's quite a bargain! Shipping and handling is just 50¢ per book in the U.S. and 75¢ per book in Canada.* I understand that accepting the 2 free books and gifts places me under no obligation to buy anything. I can always return a shipment and cancel at any time. Even if I never buy another book, the two free books and gifts are mine to keep forever.

246/349 HDN F4ZY

Name _____ (PLEASE PRINT) _____

Address _____ Apt. # _____

City _____ State/Prov. _____ Zip/Postal Code _____

Signature (if under 18, a parent or guardian must sign)

Mail to the Harlequin® Reader Service:
IN U.S.A.: P.O. Box 1867, Buffalo, NY 14240-1867
IN CANADA: P.O. Box 609, Fort Erie, Ontario L2A 5X3

Want to try two free books from another line?
Call 1-800-873-8635 or visit www.ReaderService.com.

* Terms and prices subject to change without notice. Prices do not include applicable taxes. Sales tax applicable in N.Y. Canadian residents will be charged applicable taxes. Offer not valid in Quebec. This offer is limited to one order per household. Not valid for current subscribers to Harlequin Historical books. All orders subject to credit approval. Credit or debit balances in a customer's account(s) may be offset by any other outstanding balance owed by or to the customer. Please allow 4 to 6 weeks for delivery. Offer available while quantities last.

Your Privacy—The Harlequin® Reader Service is committed to protecting your privacy. Our Privacy Policy is available online at www.ReaderService.com or upon request from the Harlequin Reader Service.

We make a portion of our mailing list available to reputable third parties that offer products we believe may interest you. If you prefer that we not exchange your name with third parties, or if you wish to clarify or modify your communication preferences, please visit us at www.ReaderService.com/consumerschoice or write to us at Harlequin Reader Service Preference Service, P.O. Box 9062, Buffalo, NY 14269. Include your complete name and address.

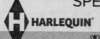
*Visit Edinburgh with Ann Lethbridge and fall for
rugged rogue Logan—the notorious Gilvry brothers
are the hottest Highlanders around!*

"She held still, as if she had not noticed the growing
warmth in the room. The heat between them. And then he
lifted her hand in his, carefully, as if it could be broken by
his greater strength. Eyes fixed on her face, he turned it over
and, bending his head, touched his lips to her palm. A warm
velvety brush of his mouth against sensitive skin. A whisper
of hot breath. Sensual. Melting.

Her insides clenched. Her heart stopped, then picked up
with a jolt and an uneven rhythm. She felt like a girl again,
all hot and bothered and unsure. And full of such longings.
Such desires.

But the woman inside her knew better. She craved all
that kiss offered. The heat. The bliss. Carnal things that
shamed her. Things she had resolved never to want again.
They left her vulnerable. A challenge she could not let go
unanswered. To do so would be to admit he had touched
her somehow.

"Charity," he said softly, as he lifted his head to look at
her, still cradling her hand in his large warm one, his thumb
gently stroking. "Never in my life have I met a woman like
you."

The words rang with truth. And they pleased her. She
leaned closer and touched her lips to his, let them linger,
cling softly, urging him to respond. And he did. Gently at
first, with care, as if he thought she might take offence or

be frightened. Then more forcefully, his mouth moving against hers as he angled his head, his free hand coming up to cradle her nape while the other retained its hold. The feel of his lips sent little thrills spiraling outward from low in her belly. On a gasp she opened her mouth and, with little licks and tastes and deep rumbling groans in his chest, he explored her. The gentleness of it was her undoing.

The way he delved and plundered her mouth as if making the discovery for the very first time was incredibly alluring. If she didn't know better, she might have thought this was his first time. Passion hummed in her veins. Dizzied her mind. Sent her tumbling into a blaze of desire.

He drew back, his chest rising and falling as if he, too, could not breathe, his gaze searching her face. And she melted in the heat in his eyes.

Has this bad boy Highlander finally met his match with English bad girl Charity? This time around, two wrongs could just make a right….

Don't miss
FALLING FOR THE HIGHLAND ROGUE
by Ann Lethbridge, out December 2013,
only in Harlequin® Historical!

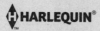

HARLEQUIN

HISTORICAL

Where love is timeless

COMING IN DECEMBER 2013

Not Just A Wallflower
by Carole Mortimer

Enigmatic beauty Ellie Rosewood is the talk of the ton. Her appointed guardian, Justin, Duke of Royston, has one job—to find Miss Rosewood a husband. But confirmed rake Justin wants Ellie all for himself!

With her coming out a huge success, Ellie is overwhelmed by the attention of London's most eligible bachelors. She finds an unexpected haven in the company of the arrogant Justin, and he begins to discover there is more to this unworldly wallflower than first appears....

A Season of Secrets
A lady never tells...

Available wherever books and ebooks are sold.

HH29764